T0329288

"NO MORE BLASPHEMY . . ."

"Just listen to me," Sarah panted, dropping to her knees. She stabbed her hand at the scroll. "There's a date right here: March 27, 1999. How would somebody in ancient Israel know about a date in the modern calendar?"

Ibrahim gazed at her a moment, then sighed and shook his head. "Sarah, do you realize that you sound like a madwoman?"

"*Me?*" she cried. "What about *you?* Is what I'm saying any crazier than that stuff about the hidden Imam and the End of Days and—"

"Be quiet!" he barked. "I will hear no more blasphemy!" He snapped his fingers twice.

Uh-oh. Sarah knew what *that* meant: The guards were being summoned. In a panic she reached for the scroll's handles—and found the blade of a scimitar at her neck.

"Wait!" she gasped. "Don't . . ."

But the sharp, cold metal pressed into her skin, silencing her. The force of it wasn't enough to puncture the flesh or draw blood; it was just enough to cause some discomfort—a hint of the *real* pain it could deliver. She remained paralyzed, watching helplessly as the other guard gathered the scroll into his arms.

The color drained from her face.

"I'm confiscating that *junk,*" Ibrahim stated disdainfully.

About the Author

Daniel Parker is the author of over twenty books for children and young adults. He lives in New York City with his wife, a dog, and a psychotic cat named Bootsie. He is a Leo. When he isn't writing, he is tirelessly traveling the world on a doomed mission to achieve rock-and-roll stardom. As of this date, his musical credits include the composition of bluegrass sound-track numbers for the film *The Grave* (starring a bloated Anthony Michael Hall) and a brief stint performing live rap music to baffled Filipino audiences in Hong Kong. Mr. Parker once worked in a cheese shop. He was fired.

COUNT DOWN

MARCH

by
Daniel Parker

Simon & Schuster
www.SimonSays.com/countdown/

First Aladdin Paperbacks edition January 1999

Produced by 17th Street Productions,
a division of Daniel Weiss Associates, Inc.

Cover design by Mike Rivilis

Aladdin Paperbacks
An imprint of Simon & Schuster
Children's Publishing Division
1230 Avenue of the Americas
New York, NY 10020

The text of this book was set in 10.5 point Rotis Serif.
Printed and bound in the United States of America
10 9 8 7 6 5 4 3 2 1

Library of Congress Cataloging-in-Publication Data
Parker, Daniel, 1970-
March / by Daniel Parker. — 1st Aladdin Paperbacks ed.
p.   cm. — (Countdown ; 3)
Summary: After everyone on Earth over twenty dies, the agents of the awakened Demon Lilith plot to destroy the Visionaries, the special teenagers who have the power to destroy her.
ISBN 0-689-81821-1 (pbk.)
[1. Supernatural—Fiction.] I. Title. II. Series: Parker, Daniel, 1970-
Countdown ; 3.
PZ7.P2198Mar   1999
[Fic]—dc21   98-46984
CIP   AC
ISBN: 978-1-4814-2588-9

To Lacey

MARCH

The Ancient Scroll
of the Scribes:

In the third lunar cycle,
During the months of Adar and Nisan
In the year 5759,
The Chosen One is cast adrift,
still separated from her brother.
Lost but not lost, alone but not alone.
As she struggles to find her way
the Seers struggle with her.
The light of the sun
will not see the earth
And so the Seers will not see
the light of truth.
Waters will rise—
from north to south,
from east to west.
The Demon will wreak havoc
upon the lands and seas ...
And the servants of the Demon
will bring death wherever they tread.

To be heavenly raises us.
Deals make it safer
for all fools to read lips.
Three twenty-seven ninety-nine.

The countdown has started. . . .

The long sleep is over.

For three thousand years I have patiently watched and waited. The Prophecies foretold the day when the sun would reach out and touch the earth—when my slumber would end, when my ancient weapon would breathe, when my dormant glory would blaze once more upon the planet and its people.

That day has arrived.

But there can be no triumph without a battle. Every civilization tells the same story. Good requires evil; redemption requires sin. The legends are as varied as are the civilizations that spawned them— yet each contains that same nugget of truth.

So I am not alone. The Chosen One awaits me. The flare opened the inner eyes of the Visionaries, those who can join the Chosen One to prevent my reign. But in order for them to defeat me, they must first make sense of their visions.

For you see, every vision is a piece of a puzzle, a puzzle that will eventually form a picture . . . a picture that I will shatter into a billion pieces and reshape in the image of my choosing.

I am prepared. My servants knew of this day. They made the necessary preparations to confuse the Visionaries—all in anticipation of that glorious time when the countdown ends and my ancient weapon ushers in the New Era.

My servants unleashed the plague that reduced the earth's population to a scattered horde of frightened adolescents. None of these children know how or why their elders and youngers perished.

And that was only the beginning.

My servants have descended upon the chaos. They will subvert the Prophecies in order to convert the masses into unknowing slaves. They will hunt down the Visionaries, one by one, until all are dead. They will eliminate the descendants of the Scribes so that none of the Visionaries will learn of the scroll. The hidden codes shall remain hidden. Terrible calamities and natural disasters will wreak havoc upon the earth. Even the Chosen One will be helpless against me.

I *will* triumph.

PART 1:

March 1–March 8, 1999

The Third Lunar Cycle

Naamah splashed down the concrete catwalk toward a waiting helicopter. Her black robe was drenched from a night of incessant rain. She was aching and exhausted from the task that Lilith had demanded of her—yet she had rarely been more joyful, more proud of a single accomplishment. It had taken twelve straight hours—twelve hours of toiling alone in the darkness and thunder—but she had done it.

She had planted nine synchronized time bombs on the Aswan High Dam—each with an explosive power of one hundred pounds of TNT.

A flood of unfathomable proportions was poised to strike.

The pounding rhythm of the helicopter's blades sliced through the downpour, rattling Naamah's bones and ears. Yet before she boarded, she paused and allowed herself one more peek at the awesome structure. It was truly magnificent: a two-mile expanse of concrete and metal that towered high above the Nile

River, an engineering marvel that provided electricity for nearly all of Egypt.

It was almost a shame to have to destroy it. . . .

She smiled.

No. The beauty of blowing this dam to pieces at such a strategic moment filled her with an ecstasy she'd never known, not even when she had led the attack on the Russian base. It was a perfect move, a checkmate—as if the entire planet had become Lilith's chessboard. After one last satisfied look she ducked under the whirling blades and jumped into the dry warmth of the passenger seat.

"Let's go," she commanded.

The pilot nodded, his wan face a mask of fear and submission. Naamah sneered contemptuously. Captain Hillerman was one of the few "adults" whom the Lilum had spared for practical purposes: a forty-year-old English pilot who had tasted the plague for the briefest instant—then been left to live as a virtual zombie, a servant of Lilith's cause. He had to know that his days were numbered. He had to know that Naamah would withdraw the antidote as soon as his duties as slave and escort were finished.

But not yet. She would do so only when the Lilum had no more need for him. She would do so only when the Prophecies had run their course, when the countdown to Lilith's rule had ended.

Timing was key.

As the helicopter began a slow climb into the rain Naamah stared down at the dull gray surface of Lake Nasser, the huge artificial reservoir created by the dam. The ancient ruins of Kalabsha Temple stood on the southern horizon, obscured by mist and cloud cover.

The view was fitting. The temple had been built in the days when Lilith had roamed the earth in human form. And soon she would roam again.

"How much time do we have?" Captain Hillerman asked anxiously.

"Relax," Naamah murmured. "We're perfectly safe."

Yes, timing was key. The Lilum would be safe from this day forward. The captain had no idea why, of course. He had no idea that the bombs had been timed to detonate nearly four weeks from now, to coincide exactly with a terrible and cataclysmic event hidden in the Prophecy Codes. . . .

CHAPTER ONE

**University of Texas Hospital,
Austin, Texas
Morning of March 1**

"Pssst. Harold. Wake up."

Dr. Harold Wurf moaned. There was an irksome buzzing in his ear. He rolled over in bed to get away from it. His head . . . He felt as if somebody were pounding it with a rubber mallet.

"Psst." A girl's clammy hand shook his bare shoulder. "Harold."

"Whah?" he croaked irritably. His mouth had the consistency of an old, wrung-out washcloth.

"You've gotta wake up."

Harold opened one eyelid—just one. *Too bright!* The sun-drenched hospital room was a brilliant white, all gleaming linen and plastic, pill bottles and cups strewn everywhere. He had a sudden flash: last night, in here, washing down ten-milligram caplets of Dexedrine with . . . was it cognac? Yes, cognac. Some floozy brought it as an "offering." Lord, what had he been *thinking?* He couldn't face the memory. Not in his condition. The eyelid closed.

"C'mon, Harold!"

He pulled the covers over his head. *Larissa.* Yes . . . that was her name. It floated up from the murky, pounding recesses of his poisoned brain. Luscious Larissa. Blond and beautiful. The first one he'd saved. The first one of far too many. Now if only she would shut her mouth. How could her southern accent have been so sexy last night and be so horrid this morning?

"They're calling for you, Harold," she murmured. She shook him again. "They're gettin' impatient."

Gettin' impatien'. He moaned once more, disgusted with the girl's voice, this hospital, everything. He had to face the mob. *Again.* He had to face those hundreds of poor idiots who thought he was sent here from above—all those lonely teenagers desperate to be fed, desperate to be reassured, desperate to be healed.

Who cared if they were impatient? What about him? *He* could use some comforting, too. He still wasn't any closer to figuring out a cure for the plague that had instantly melted everyone over the age of twenty-one. And he knew that time was running out. He himself was already twenty.

"Harold?"

No, it wasn't *his* fault that every survivor in Austin believed he had magic powers. So he'd gotten lucky a couple of dozen times with some nausea medication. But those kids were all the same: spreading rumors, exaggerating the truth, making him out to be some kind of messiah.

"C'mon, Harold. Please—"

"I'm up!" he barked.

There was a moment of silence. He suddenly realized he was naked. Christ, he was a mess.

"I'm sorry," she whispered. "What can I do to help?"

"Help? Go to the medicine closet down the hall. Bring me two bottles of Ritalin and a package marked Methylene-dioxymethamphetamine. *That* will help."

Sniff, sniff.
Ka-ching!
A million flashbulbs went off in Harold's frontal lobe; a million slot machines whirled and hit the jackpot.

"Whew!" he breathed. Now *there* was a jump start!

He lifted his head. The hot white powder burned the inside of his nose. There was a tickle in the back of his throat. He blinked and glanced around the hospital room, reeling with wonder at how *crisp* everything looked, how *clear*. His headache was gone. He was filled with a giddy euphoria. It was a new day! Time to face his flock!

"Harold, I think we better go downstairs. A bunch of kids are waiting in the cafeteria. They're gonna start comin' up soon if we don't hurry."

Harold's eyes darted to Larissa. She was standing barefoot by the door in a white bathrobe, her long blond hair flowing past her shoulders, her smooth skin flushed. A smile crossed his face. She looked *good*. Beautiful, in fact. And he could have her. She thought he had the divine gift of healing. In a way, he did. After all, he'd already saved a hundred lives. He was a genius, a doctor, a savior.

She cast a furtive glance at him, then blushed and lowered her eyes, smiling shyly.

"What are you looking at?" she whispered.

9

"Come here," he commanded. His voice was thick. He placed the tiny makeup mirror lined with alternate rows of powdered Ritalin and MDMA on the night table. "Now."

Her smile widened. "But the kids—"

"They aren't going anywhere, Larissa," he interrupted. "Believe me."

Harold floated at the vague edges of a fading dream. He was happy. He was playing ball with Pop outside the main house . . . he could see the wheat field . . . the old, familiar red barn in the distance. But something was wrong. Something was coming from *outside* himself, his world—rattling, hammering.

"Open up!" a voice shouted.

The dream was gone.

Harold grunted. The hammering grew louder. He wasn't asleep anymore. No—he was in bed, under the covers, arms and legs entwined with Larissa. His eyes opened. Somebody was knocking on the door. *Loudly.*

"Open up! I know you're in there!"

Harold frowned. It was a boy, but he didn't recognize the voice. It must be a newcomer, one of the recent arrivals who didn't fully believe in Harold's all-encompassing powers. That would explain the rude tone. The boy would believe soon enough, though. Harold extracted himself from Larissa's limbs and sat up in bed.

There was another knock. The door vibrated on its hinges. "Open this—"

"Wait downstairs with the others," Harold interrupted.

"I can't wait!" the voice yelled. "People are sick! We're running out of food!"

Oh, please, Harold thought tiredly, rubbing his bloodshot eyes. Sick? He'd wager that a few kids had the sniffles, and all the newcomers thought it was a major crisis. Of course, the cafeteria refrigerators *were* empty . . . but even so, there was nothing *he* could do about it. Why did these kids think *everything* was his responsibility?

Larissa yawned. "What's going on?" she murmured. She shifted in bed, then stretched and glanced up at him.

"They need me downstairs," Harold grumbled. "They're worried they're going to starve." A bitter laugh escaped his lips. "I guess I have to conjure bread out of thin air, right?"

Larissa stared at him with an expression of utter blankness. Harold sighed. Poor Larissa. Gorgeous, but dumb as a bedpan. She probably had no idea what the word *conjure* meant.

The door rattled again. "Come out here!" the voice insisted. Much to Harold's surprise, Larissa bolted up beside him in bed.

"Harold will be out in a minute," she called, wide-awake. "He needs to get himself ready. Tell the others that there's going to be plenty of food. Harold has a plan for all of us. He's going to feed us."

Harold's eyes narrowed. *No, no, no.* What was she *saying?*

But Larissa just stared back at him with a

11

worshipful gaze—completely void of any humor, irony, or sarcasm.

"That *is* your divine plan, isn't it, Harold?" she asked.

An hour later Harold emerged alone from a leisurely shower, pulled on his green doctor's pajamas, and collapsed on the empty bed.

He felt as if he were about to vomit.

I'm screwed. Completely, totally, 100 percent screwed.

Thanks to Larissa, a volatile and angry teenage rabble was now waiting for him. And many of them—*most* of them—believed that he would miraculously produce a wondrous feast. What would they do if he failed? Would they turn on him? Would they kill him?

Find a solution! he commanded himself.

But he couldn't. For the first time in his life, fear interfered with his normally flawless thought processes.

Well, at least he'd learned one important lesson. He couldn't afford to let his guard down with Larissa anymore. He couldn't joke with her—because she was the most devoted fanatic of all. She truly believed he had saved her life with a divine hand.

What could he possibly do?

His eyes wandered over to the mirror on the night table. One last fat line of MDMA lay waiting—with a crisp, rolled-up five-dollar bill by its side. He licked his lips, then leaned over and snorted it up in one breath.

12

Whoosh . . .

He sniffed a few times, blinking rapidly. For a moment he studied his reflection in the tiny mirror. His penetrating blue eyes gazed back at him through the powdery white residue. He'd lost some weight, hadn't he? It served him well. His dark, wavy hair had grown all the way to his collarbone, and his sharp jaw was covered with a week's worth of stubble. He looked rugged, handsome, sinewy—a wild man of the mountains, like a biblical prophet. No wonder they worshiped him.

He sat up straight.

Clarity. Yes, yes. He was thinking now. He could handle this situation. His mind hummed like a silicon processor, the millions of synapses firing in perfect concert to examine every last bit of data, every last experience. . . .

Aha!

The solution was already there. It had come to him this morning. In a dream, no less!

Home.

Of course. The old farm, up in the Texas Panhandle, just outside of Amarillo. It was perfect for housing and feeding his flock. What with a decent-sized house, a barn, a silo, five hundred acres . . . it had to be deserted, too—

Ma and Pop are gone.

He swallowed once, his throat caught by the sudden realization. He'd been so busy since the melting plague started that he hadn't even had time to wonder what was going on outside the hospital. Ma and Pop had surely vaporized; after all, they weren't teenagers.

He thrust the thought from his mind. He couldn't dwell on thoughts of his parents. Time was too precious. Unless he wanted to end up dead like them, he had to focus on his own survival. He wasn't a teenager anymore, either. It was only a matter of time before the plague caught up with him.

Anyway, the farm was perfect. Pop had always stockpiled tons of foodstuffs there: wheat and corn and vegetables and cattle. Harold could even turn the main house into a makeshift lab to work on finding a cure for the plague. He had all the materials he needed right here. His hopes soared. Food and shelter for everyone! A cure! Why hadn't he thought of this before? The timing was uncanny, unreal. It was almost . . . a sign.

Maybe they're right about me. Maybe I am connected to some higher power.

There was a soft knock on the door. "Harold? They can't wait any—"

"Coming, Larissa!" he cried, leaping gleefully out of bed. He threw open the door and marched out into the hall.

Dozens and dozens of smelly and disheveled kids were waiting for him. *My flock!* They were packed into the hallway all the way down to the elevator—staring at him in silence, their grubby faces a mix of hope, anger, and apprehension.

"I have a plan," he announced. His voice boomed down to the very last listener. "It came to me in a dream. A vision! We're packing our belongings. All of us—the weak, the sick, and the hungry. Help your brothers and sisters. I've seen a place.

14

I'm taking you home." The mystical BS flowed out of his mouth as smoothly as chocolate syrup out of a spout. It was such a blast, a *rush*. These people were focused on his every word, their initially dubious expressions melting away with wonder. His tone grew ecstatic.

"It's a holy pilgrimage! A march north to the promised land!"

CHAPTER TWO

Sarah Levy was caught in a bizarre netherworld between life and death. She lay on her back, wrapped in cool silk sheets—on an enormous bed that sat in a vast, dark stone chamber. She heard a noise, a kind of steady drumming . . . like rain. Yes. She remembered something about rain, didn't she? She searched her memory, but the images were distant and unformed, like flashes just outside her vision. . . .

A damp breeze tickled her face. She tried to sit up, but her weakened body wouldn't allow it. Two girls, their faces concealed by black cloth, stood by her side. She wanted to ask them where she was, only she was far too tired. . . .

Ice-cold water dribbled past her lips, down over her tongue, soothing her dry throat. The hooded girls loomed over her. Once again Sarah wondered if she were already dead. She gulped thirstily, eyes half closed, wondering when this strange purgatory would end and she would see the next world. Or maybe this *was* the next world. It would be so ironic, wouldn't it? She was the sole atheist in a

16

devoutly religious family, and now she had proof that there *was* an afterlife.

Unfortunately the joke was on her—because the price of that proof was death.

She *had* to be dead. She'd been attacked by Arab nomads in the middle of the desert. The memories were growing clearer. The last thing she remembered was that one of the nomads had charged right at her on his horse.

But why was she alone? Where was her granduncle Elijah? Her mom and dad? Had they already gone on to some better place?

Night had come. The room was dark. Seemingly endless rain continued to pound outside the open window, dripping onto the floor. Sarah was surprised that there would be rain in heaven, but what did she know? She'd always imagined that the weather in the next life would be perfect and static, never changing—not that she had ever thought much about it.

She glanced around the bed. In the dim light she caught a glimpse of the tag on one of the sheets. Ralph Lauren. She almost laughed out loud. Not only were there rainy nights in heaven, but there were expensive designers as well.

The following morning Sarah felt much stronger.

Her mind was alert. Hunger picked at her stomach. She sat up in bed.

Raindrops continued to splatter on the windowsill. The puddle on the floor was growing. Even without her glasses, Sarah could see that the room was very

17

sparsely decorated: No pictures hung on the smooth stone walls; no curtains adorned the one open window. There was a beautiful Persian rug stitched with a flowery red pattern that lay between the bed and the open door and an intricate wooden chandelier that hung from the ceiling. But aside from that there was nothing else, not even a nightstand or dresser.

This isn't heaven.

No—of course it wasn't. She didn't even *believe* in heaven.

So where was she?

Her pulse picked up a beat. Okay. She'd been semidelirious for a while. Exactly how long, she didn't know—maybe a couple of days. But this was *not* the time to panic. She had to be cool. Cool and detached. Just the way she'd learned in journalism school. She had to find out *where* she was, *why* she was here, and *how* she could get out.

After another quick study of her surroundings she found her wire-rim frames lying on one of the silky pillows beside her. She pulled them on, tossed aside the sheets, and tottered over to the window—trying her best to avoid getting wet. Her legs were still a little shaky, but they could carry her weight. If necessary, they could carry her all the way back to Jerusalem. . . .

Good Lord!

The window was perched in a high tower. *Really* high. She shoved her head out into the rain, glancing in amazement to her right and left. An intricate complex of massive stone spires and turrets greeted her unbelieving eyes. Her shoulders were soaked in an

18

instant, but she hardly noticed. What *was* this place? From what she could see, it looked like some kind of Middle Eastern medieval castle, something out of *The Arabian Nights*. Her room was probably a hundred feet off the desert floor, if not more.

Only . . . the land beneath the building wasn't desert.

It was an oasis.

Spread below her was a perfectly symmetrical square of the richest, most lush greenery she had ever seen—smack in the middle of the barren plain. The fields stretched off into the stormy distance and suddenly stopped at the damp sand, as if a giant green square had been painted on a flat yellow-gray floor. The whole scene was mind-boggling. . . .

Sarah shook the water from her limp brown hair and ducked back inside, wiping her glasses with the sleeve of her pajamas. Her breath started coming fast. She didn't even *own* pajamas. Whose were these? What the—

"Do you like what you see?" a deep voice asked.

Sarah whirled around.

A handsome young Arab man stood smiling in the arched doorway.

Whoa.

He was *more* than handsome, actually. He could have been a model: olive skin, deep black eyes, black wavy hair—and such perfectly white teeth and strong cheekbones that they almost looked fake. He wore a loose-fitting, collarless white shirt with trousers to match, but it was obvious that the baggy clothes hid a lean and muscular frame.

19

He strolled over to the window and stood beside her, gazing out to the field.

Sarah couldn't take her eyes off him. She couldn't even *speak*.

"Look at this rain," the stranger breathed. He spoke with a mild trace of an accent—but it was British, not Middle Eastern. "A miracle and a blessing. If this keeps up, I'll have to disconnect the aqueducts and irrigation systems. We'll be flooded."

Sarah shook her head, utterly bewildered. "Where are we?" she found herself asking.

"My home."

Her jaw dropped. "You *live* here?" she gasped.

He shrugged, smiling humbly, then turned to her. "So do you. This is your home, too. All that you see belongs to you."

Sarah gaped at him. *My home, too?* That made absolutely no sense. She tried to swallow, but her mouth was suddenly bone dry.

"I know you must be confused, Sarah," the stranger said soothingly. "Don't worry. There will be plenty of time to—"

"How do you know my name?" she interrupted. Her voice dropped to a hoarse croak. "Who *are* you?"

"Forgive me." He lowered his eyes. "I am Ibrahim Al-Saif. I know your name because I looked through your belongings. It was wrong to do so, but you see, I had to learn . . . I had to learn everything about you."

Sarah's thoughts began to race. Terrible connections formed: This stranger had an English accent, like the girls who'd blown her granduncle's home in Israel to bits. Like the girls who wanted Elijah's scroll, the ancient scroll he told Sarah about right before he melted into a puddle of black goo. This guy knew her identity. So did those girls. And the girls in *this* place also wore black.

He's one of them!

She took a step back, panicked. Her eyes flashed to her knapsack, lying on the floor by her bed. The scroll was still inside. The stranger said he'd looked through her belongings. So *he* must have been after the scroll, too. How many people even *knew* about that crumbling parchment—about the ancient prophecies, about the mysterious codes supposedly hidden within? Were they *that* important?

"You want the scroll, don't you?" she whispered. "Don't you?"

His face fell. He shook his head. "Wh-what do you mean?" he stammered.

"You tell *me!*" Sarah spat.

"Sarah, I don't even read Hebrew," he protested. "What could I possibly want with an old Hebrew scroll?"

Sarah's eyes darted to the window. She couldn't jump; it was far too high. And *he* blocked the path to the doorway.

"Listen to me, Sarah," he murmured urgently. "I don't want that scroll—I don't want any of your belongings. I only want *you.*"

She gazed at him, shuddering. "What are you *talking* about? Why are you acting like you know me? You don't!"

"Try to understand," he pleaded. "Your face—it came to me in a vision. I knew you'd come. I knew I had to

21

save you. First from the desert, and later from the ocean. Every day, from sunrise to sunset, my stable boys and I would ride through the desert—searching. Then Allah showed us the footprints, blessed be the All-Merciful. Those beautiful footprints in the sand. We followed them straight to you. And the moment we found you, the heavens opened up, showering us with this miraculous rain. . . . It was a sign. A sign from Allah."

Sarah simply stared at him, unable to process what she'd just heard. It sounded like gibberish. She had only one inane thought: *So this must be the guy who charged me before I passed out.*

"You're my desert angel," he murmured. "My desert angel. Don't you understand? It's Allah's will. We were meant to be together."

"No," Sarah breathed. She wanted desperately to move—but she was far too petrified. "Shut up. Stop it."

He shook his head, then stepped forward and took her hands in his own. "But I love you, Sarah Levy. And I'm going to love you for all time."

**Outskirts of Springfield,
Illinois
Night of March 5**

Is this storm ever going to end? Julia Morrison wondered.

She squirmed in the passenger seat of the rickety old pickup truck. She was stiff from another long day of driving at about ten miles an hour, and she was getting antsy. Nights were the worst. It was almost impossible to see the road. The weak yellow headlights hardly penetrated the rain. And there was a perpetual waterfall over the windows, almost like a curtain. With each swipe of the windshield wipers the curtain would part for a split second—and then it would close again. The rapid, uneven rhythm reminded her of a grandfather clock: *ticktock, ticktock.* . . .

"Brother," George Porter groaned from the driver's seat. "Is this rain ever gonna end?"

Julia managed a faint smile. "I was thinking the exact same thing," she murmured. It was funny: She and George *always* seemed to be thinking the exact same thing, or saying the same thing at the same time . . . or enjoying a nice long spell of silence. Like Julia, George truly appreciated the value of being quiet. Julia would have never guessed in a million years that

23

she had something in common with a sixteen-year-old punk who dyed his hair platinum blond and partied like a rock star—but she was wrong. They had plenty in common. Plenty.

"Whatcha thinking now?" George asked.

Julia shrugged.

"You know what *I'm* thinking?" he said. His voice was flat. "I'm thinking that we've been driving for almost two weeks through this freaking rain, and I still don't feel any safer."

Julia nodded. She stole a quick peek at George through the long, matted brown curls that hung in her eyes. Her hair was disgusting. With all the moisture, she was starting to grow dreadlocks. If she didn't take a shower soon, she would look like a Rastafarian, like a female Ziggy Marley. What did it matter, though? It wasn't as if she had to impress anybody—

"You don't think those chicks could have followed us, do you?" George blurted.

She shook her head. "No way." But the words just popped out of her mouth; she didn't really believe them. Ever since they'd escaped from those crazy girls back in Jackson, Ohio, Julia hadn't felt safe for a second. *I guess when someone threatens to kill you, you don't get over it very easily,* she thought.

But she didn't want to admit she was still afraid. She wanted to reassure George—and herself. "If they followed us, they'd have caught up by now."

"Yeah, they probably wouldn't bother," George mumbled after a moment. He was hunched over the wheel, his green eyes slitted, his bony knuckles a chalky white.

24

Julia nodded, swallowing. She wanted to agree with him. But how could she possibly know what those girls would do? She didn't even know who they were—other than a bunch of psychopaths who wanted to kill her and George because they both had visions. . . .

But the girls weren't her biggest worry. Far more terrifying—to her, at least—was the fact that Luke was still at large. Because if anyone would chase after them, *he* would. His words still burned in her mind: *"If you ever try to run away again, I'll kill you."* He'd meant it. She didn't even want to *think* about what Luke would do to George. George was tough, but he still had no idea how sick or dangerous Luke could be. No idea.

"You know, I wonder what happened to Luke," George muttered. "I hope he's dead. I hope those crazy bitches killed him."

Julia stared at him. *Did he know that I was thinking about Luke, too?* For a moment she was struck once more by the strange coincidence—the uncanny sensation that the two of them shared something like ESP. But it faded . . . and she was swept up in a whirlwind of conflicting emotions: anger at George for wishing Luke was dead, anger at *herself* for wishing Luke was dead, self-pity and self-hatred for the three long years she'd wasted with Luke . . . and finally relief, blessed relief, that Luke was *gone,* out of her life forever, a memory.

"Julia?" George cast her a sidelong glance. "I didn't offend you or anything, did I?"

"No," she said. But she was grateful that he asked. In all the days of being alone with him in this pickup truck, she'd grown sensitive to his moods. Usually

George acted unafraid, gruff, uncaring—older and more jaded than any sixteen-year-old she'd ever met. But every now and then a crack in the shell would appear, and she would catch a brief glimpse of someone else: somebody vulnerable, compassionate . . . and oddly endearing.

"You sure?" George asked.

Julia nodded. "Yeah. I just—I don't know. I just hope I never see Luke again. Ever." She paused. "But I know I won't," she added, mostly to convince herself.

George remained silent.

"Think we should pull over soon?" he asked after a minute. "I'm pretty sure I saw a sign back there for Springfield. I bet we can find a place to crash, like a hotel or something. . . ." His voice faded. He hunched over the wheel, his eyes narrowing. "Hey—you see that?"

Julia peered into the onslaught of rain. Yes, she *did* see something. Somewhere ahead was a flat, triangular red blur. *Lights.*

"I think there are cars up there," George breathed.

Julia strained her eyes as the blur drew closer, leaning so far forward that her nose nearly touched the glass. George was right. She could see two long rows of taillights that stretched into the distance and met on the horizon.

Wow. Was it her imagination—or were there *lots* of cars?

And none of them seemed to be moving.

"You see that?" George asked again. He sounded excited. He jerked a finger off to the right side of the highway, then downshifted. "Look over there!"

Julia gasped. Hovering above the tree line were

26

several glowing towers, faint and ghostly in the rain. Her heart bounced. She was staring at something very, very familiar, wasn't she? Familiar and long forgotten. A city skyline.

No. Could it be?

City lights, stalled traffic—that meant only one thing. Civilization. She swallowed. She hadn't seen another human being besides George since they'd escaped Jackson. It would be so nice to talk to somebody, *anybody*. But no, no . . . she shouldn't let herself get worked up; she shouldn't set herself up for a disappointment. She glanced down and found she was rubbing her moist palms on her jeans. Maybe Springfield was somehow spared the plague. Maybe everything was normal here. Maybe there were even adults still alive.

"*Look* at all those cars, Julia!" George cried, laughing. "Look at 'em!"

"I know," she whispered, gazing at the swiftly approaching mass of lights. "I know."

George hit the brakes, nearly slamming into the back of a Range Rover. "I'm gonna see what's up," he mumbled.

Before Julia could answer, George threw open the door and popped out into the rain. He left the engine running. He didn't even bother to close the door behind him.

Julia fumbled with her seat belt. "George!" she shouted over the downpour. "Wait!" The buckle finally snapped apart, and she flung open her door and jumped out onto the pavement. Her feet were instantly drenched. She didn't care. She heard George talking to somebody, but it was raining so hard that she couldn't see a thing.

27

People! Human beings! She covered her head with her hands and plowed into the darkness, splashing with every step.

The back door of the Range Rover was open. A hand yanked her inside. The door slammed—and Julia slid onto a velvety cushion next to George.

She found herself staring at two teenage boys.

More kids?

A strange disappointment overcame her. She'd been hoping to see a grown-up. Somebody responsible. Proof that everything was normal. She was just so *sick* of seeing kids her age, kids who didn't know how to take care of themselves in the first place.

The boys smiled at her from the front seat.

Well, at least they seemed friendly. And both of them were relatively healthy: Their eyes were bright; they had color in their cheeks; they wore shiny yellow raincoats that could have been brand-new. They *looked* normal. But then, so had those girls from Jackson.

The inside of the car was perfectly quiet except for the hammering of rain on the roof.

"Isn't this rain wild?" the boy in the driver's seat finally asked. He shook his head. "I've never seen anything like it."

"Yeah, me neither," George piped up. "It's crazy."

"Where are you coming from?" the boy in the passenger seat asked.

"Pittsburgh," George answered. "By the way, I'm George."

"My name's Ted," the driver said.

"Bob," the passenger put in.

28

There was a silence. It took Julia a moment to realize that everyone was waiting for her to state her name. "Oh—sorry. Julia," she murmured awkwardly. She forced a smile.

"So where are you guys from?" George asked.

Bob flashed a rueful grin. "Chicago. Or what's left of it."

George hesitated. "What do you mean?"

"Half the city's already underwater," Ted answered. "The rain is really heavy up there. Lake Michigan totally flooded." He laughed. "But hey—what are you gonna do? Compared to some other things, it's no big deal. Where are you guys headed?"

Julia didn't answer. She could feel her smile grow strained. No big deal that Lake Michigan had completely flooded Chicago? What *was* a big deal?

"Are you going to Springfield?" Bob asked. "A lot of people are."

All of a sudden Julia didn't feel so chatty. It was a relief to have contact with people—but she didn't feel like revealing any information about herself or where she was going. Besides, she and George had no idea who these boys were. None at all.

"You going somewhere else?" Ted pressed, looking at George.

George brushed his stringy blond hair aside and glanced at Julia.

"We don't know where we're headed," she and George both said at the same time.

Julia bit her lip—but she couldn't help smiling again. *ESP,* she thought. *I know it.*

"So what's up with the traffic jam?" George asked,

not so subtly trying to change the subject. "Why are all the cars stopped?"

Ted shrugged. "We're not sure. It's been this way for a couple of hours. My guess is that Lake Springfield flooded, too, so the highway is blocked."

George nodded. "Why is everybody trying to go to Springfield, anyway?"

"Maybe for electricity," Ted answered. "The power's out in a lot of places around here." He jerked his head toward Bob. "But we're headed out west. A bunch of our friends heard that there's somebody out there who can stop the melting plague. That's the rumor, anyway. They call him the 'Chosen One' or something . . . I don't know. Have *you* heard anything about it?"

The Chosen One!

Julia's entire body immediately tensed.

Yes, she knew about the Chosen One. She'd never seen him, or her, or whoever the Chosen One was, if it even *was* a person . . . but she knew. When the visions came, a voice whispered that the Chosen One was waiting for her, out west. But the last people she'd met, the girls from Jackson—they'd wanted to *kill* her because of her visions. Did these guys have visions, too? Or was this a trap? Were Ted and Bob just trying to trick her and George into revealing that they had visions?

Julia desperately wanted to admit that she knew about the Chosen One. She wanted to find other people who had visions, who understood her the way George did. . . .

Her eyes darted to George. He pretended to be calm. But a muscle in his jaw jumped.

30

Ted didn't seem to notice. He continued to speak—sounding more happy-go-lucky by the minute. "Anyway, we figured we'd check it out. I mean, a chosen one? It sounds crazy. But what have we got to lose? It beats sitting around and waiting to die, right?"

George lifted his shoulders. "I guess," he stated evenly. He edged toward Julia. "Well, it was nice meeting you."

Julia nodded. Panic was creeping up on her. She clasped the door handle. Her arm was shaking. She kept her eyes pinned to Ted. The Mr. Cheerful act was a little too over-the-top. Just like those girls from Jackson, the way they pretended to be so happy and carefree . . .

"You're taking off so soon?" Ted asked. "Don't you want—"

"We should really split," George interrupted. "See ya."

That was all Julia needed to hear. She threw open the door and dashed back to the truck.

"Hey!" Ted shouted after them. "Where are—" His voice was lost in the rain.

Get me out of here, Julia pleaded silently. *Just get me out of here.* The next few seconds were a blur: a series of splashes, doors slamming, the screech of tires as George threw the truck into reverse and spun around—and then they were speeding off in the direction from which they'd come . . . away from the cars, away from Springfield, into the darkness.

Julia drew in a shaky breath. Her heart thumped painfully. That had been close.

Or *had* it?

She blinked. *Hold on.* Did she even know? For

31

all she knew, those boys were telling the truth. Maybe she was just being paranoid. Maybe Ted and Bob *were* looking for the Chosen One. Maybe they were like Julia and George—compelled to go west for reasons they didn't understand, in search of answers they might never find. If they *were* real Visionaries, then Julia and George might have blown a chance to learn something important.

But in the end, did it matter? All that mattered was that she and George were safe. They couldn't afford to take risks. They couldn't afford to talk to *anyone*. No matter how desperate they grew for human contact, they needed to keep to themselves. Their lives depended on it.

"You know what I think?" George whispered after a minute. He reached over to touch her wet arm. "I think we should lay low for a while. I don't think we should try to make any new friends."

Julia took a deep breath, then shrugged and smiled. "Who needs friends?"

FOUR

**Egyptian Desert,
near El Daheir
Night of March 8**

"Allah-u-akhbar . . ."

Sarah lay sprawled across her luxurious bed, listening to the distant and alien chant of the muezzin, the Muslim holy man who summoned the faithful to prayer five times a day. Darkness had fallen over the palace and the desert estate. The sweet, lilting voice mingled with the rain in her window, creating a resonant hum that filled the whole room.

It could have been a dream.

How many times during the past few days had she felt like this—as if she were just about to wake up?

"Allah-u-akhbar," the voice droned. *"Allah . . ."*

But she wouldn't wake up. Not now, not ever.

She anxiously glanced at her journal. It sat on top of the soft sheets beside her, right next to the scroll. She slept with both of them every night. She wasn't even sure *why;* she hadn't looked at either since she'd regained consciousness five days ago. She'd been too sick, too weak, too disoriented to bother. The scroll, with all its mysteries, still terrified her. And the journal . . . well, any hope she had of keeping an unemotional record of raw data had long since vanished. Her life was too strange.

No, strange didn't even begin to describe it. Her life had entered the realm of a twisted, third-rate fairy tale.

Look at me! she thought wretchedly. She didn't even look like herself. She looked like a mummy, wrapped from head to toe in the traditional black dress of an Orthodox Islamic woman. It was absurd, insane.

Why me? Why?

A dismal laugh escaped her lips. On impulse, she reached over and snatched up her journal. Maybe she wouldn't be able to record any objective truths—but she had to write *something*.

For some reason that I can't even begin to comprehend, I wound up at the home of a guy named Ibrahim Al-Saif. He is the sole inheritor of eight estates across the globe, 119 teenage servants, and approximately $750 million. His father, Hakeem Al-Saif, was CEO and owner of United Petroleum, based in Kuwait.

Ibrahim watched his entire

34

family vaporize on New Year's Eve — his father, his mother, his two older brothers, as well as several hundred guests and servants. He was at home for the holidays. He is a student at Oxford. Or he <u>was</u>, anyway, before the flare. He speaks five languages fluently. He's only nineteen, but he acts like he's forty. He acts like a king. In a way, he <u>is</u> a king. Everybody around here treats him like one.

He is also a devout Muslim. He has nothing to do with the people who wear black robes, like I suspected at first. He honestly believes that all this rain and the flare and the plague are signs of "Qiyamah" — the Last Day. According to him, a savior is going to appear in Mecca soon, the "Imam Mahdi": a *descendant of Mohammed who is supposed to redeem the righteous on the Last Day. Ibrahim plans to go to Mecca to meet him.*

And somewhere along the way, he wants to marry <u>me</u>.

He keeps telling me he loves me. It's crazy! He doesn't even know me! I'm grateful that he saved my life, but he thinks I am some kind of mystical being and that I am destined to become his wife when the Imam Mahdi has purged the earth of sinners and

Sarah stopped writing. She stared vacantly into space.

The desire to record her thoughts rapidly dwindled—like a dying campfire on a cold, rainy day. A nauseating mix of shame and self-loathing began to engulf her instead. Here she was, contentedly writing away . . . and her brother was probably *dead*. Why had she laughed earlier? There was nothing funny about her situation. Nothing at all. She shouldn't even *be* here. She should be on her way back to

36

Jerusalem. True, she'd been weak at first, but now she was fine. She was *better* than fine. She'd never felt healthier in her whole life. Ibrahim and his servants were constantly fawning over her—preparing her sumptuous vegetarian feasts, clothing her, catering to her every whim. She'd probably gained five pounds. Last night she'd watched *Dumb and Dumber* on a VCR in one of the hundreds of rooms.

Jesus! What in God's name was she doing? Why didn't she just get up and go?

But the truth was obvious. Obvious and despicable. She *liked* it here. After two months of living on stale scraps, it felt pretty good to stuff her face with gourmet food three times a day. It wasn't so bad that a gorgeous millionaire claimed to be in love with her, either—for whatever misguided reason. And deep down, she had to admit something even more disgusting: She probably *would* have left already if Ibrahim weren't so good-looking.

"It's sick," she said out loud. *Sick.*

Her brother's thin, pale face drifted through her mind. She winced. She'd pretty much forgotten about Josh since she'd been in this place, hadn't she? He'd always told her she was selfish and self-absorbed—but this went way beyond that. What was it he'd said to her the night before the solar flare? *"I want to go home. The only reason you made me come here was because you were bored. You only think about yourself. That's the way you've always been."*

The journal and pen slipped from her fingers.

Josh is right—

There was a knock on the heavy wooden door.

"It's Ibrahim, Sarah. May I come in?"

"Yeah," she answered distractedly. She jumped out of bed and began to pace around the rug. It was actually perfect timing. She would say good-bye to Ibrahim this very instant. *Now.* She pulled off her hood and ran a shaky hand through her soft, perfumed brown hair. This bizarre little vacation was over. She was officially recovered. Time to find Josh. She would get the scroll back in his hands. *He* was smart. *He* could make sense of the prophecy, or crack the code—or *whatever* it was they were supposed to do.

She dashed back to the bed and gathered the journal and scroll up in both arms. If Josh . . .

The door swung open.

Sarah's eyes narrowed.

Ibrahim wasn't alone. Two other Arab boys stood at his side. Their faces were expressionless. Sarah glanced among the three of them. The contrast between the deadness of the boys' eyes and the sweetness of Ibrahim's smile was strange . . . and more than a little unsettling.

"What are you doing?" Ibrahim asked.

"Well, uh, actually, I . . . uh, wanted to tell you—" She broke off in midsentence, hugging the journal and scroll tightly against her chest. *Jesus.* Those other boys were wearing *swords.* Big ones. Huge, curved, shiny scimitars dangled from blue sashes tied around their white cloaks. What was going on?

Ibrahim took a step forward. "You want to run away," he stated. His smile faded.

Sarah blinked in surprise. *Run away?*

No, no. Something was very, very wrong here. She wanted to *leave*. Running away didn't mean the same thing as leaving. Running away meant *escaping*—as if she were breaking a rule, as if she had an obligation to stay. Her heart beat a little faster.

"You don't have to lie to me," he murmured. His tone was grim. "I knew this would happen. I just didn't expect it would be so soon."

"I . . . I . . . ," she breathed. Fear began to consume her. Until this moment Ibrahim had seemed weird, deluded—but never *threatening*.

"Where do you plan to go, Sarah?" Ibrahim asked. His beautiful, glittering black eyes bored into her own. "It's a wasteland out there. Don't you see that you have everything here you could possibly want?"

She took a step back. "B-but I have to find my brother," she stammered, unable to tear herself from his gaze. "I should have told you earlier. . . . See, I have to leave. I have to go to Jerusalem to get him. You don't understand. It's not that I don't appreciate everything you've done and—"

"Your brother is dead, Sarah," Ibrahim interrupted.

Sarah shook her head furiously. "That's not true."

He shrugged. "It is true. He perished along with—"

"Shut up!" she barked. "You don't know that. How would you know that?"

"I know the signs of the Last Day," Ibrahim replied matter-of-factly. His voice softened. "Your brother didn't submit to Allah. He's a nonbeliever. All the nonbelievers are dead or will be very soon."

Sarah took another step back. She couldn't stop shaking her head. "That's a load of bull!" she

39

snapped. "I'm a nonbeliever, too. I don't believe in *anything.*" But even as she lashed out at him she knew that most of her anger was directed at herself—for abandoning Josh, for the awful possibility that this warped Egyptian stranger might be right about her brother's fate. . . .

Ibrahim sighed. He jerked his head at the servant on his left. The boy lurched forward and snatched the top end of the scroll, trying to tug it from Sarah's grasp.

"Hey!" she shrieked. With a violent twist she wrenched herself free of him and tumbled back against the bed.

The boy stepped toward her. His fingers wrapped around the handle of his scimitar.

"Back off," she snarled, her chest heaving. Instinctively she tucked the scroll under her arm. Her panicked eyes darted to Ibrahim. "What are you doing? *Stop* him!"

Ibrahim frowned. He snapped his fingers twice. The boy froze in place.

"Sarah, please don't make this any more difficult than it has to be," Ibrahim stated. He sounded impatient. "You must—"

"Why are you doing this?" Sarah interrupted. Her voice dropped to a tremulous whisper. She blinked rapidly. "Why won't you let me go?"

Ibrahim smiled again—and for once it was the most horrifyingly ugly smile she had ever seen. "I'm doing this because I love you," he said.

"Stop *saying* that!" she wailed. "Why do you keep saying that?"

"Because it's the truth," he murmured. "And soon you will love me. Soon you will find your faith. But it's going to take time. You must renounce your old ways and submit."

She lowered her eyes, unable to face him, unable to listen. Her throat tightened. A single, hot tear fell across her cheek. "But I just want to leave," she breathed desperately. "Please . . ."

Ibrahim stepped across the room. "I know you want to leave," he whispered. He delicately lifted her chin with his forefinger. "But you can't. It wasn't meant to be. You're mine. You'll be with me forever, Sarah, remember? Forever."

She stared back at him through a growing haze of tears. *Forever.* The word echoed through her brain with the finality of a vault slamming shut. A final, hopeless gasp escaped her lips, like the last utterance of a drowning person. So there was no leaving this place. No amount of protest would do any good. *"You're mine."* Ibrahim's statement was meant literally. As far as he was concerned, she was his slave, his *property.*

"Please don't cry," he soothed. His hand slipped from her chin, down toward the frayed parchment under her arm. "Now, I think it would be best—"

"No, no, no!" she shouted, squirming away from him across the mattress. Even if this lunatic could imprison her, there was no *way* he would get his hands on Elijah's scroll. She gripped it so tightly that the wooden rods buckled. "This is *mine!*"

He straightened and pursed his lips. "Yes, Sarah, but it's a distraction—"

"You said you didn't want my stuff!" she yelled. "Remember? Was that a lie?"

For the briefest instant his face soured. Then he sighed and shook his head. "No, Sarah," he answered dully. "It wasn't a lie."

"Then get away from me," she spat.

He blinked once and forced a smile. "Very well, my dear. But in time, you'll see that you have no need for that scroll. In time, you'll see that my ways are truth. You *will* join me."

Before Sarah could say another word, Ibrahim and his servants strode from the room and left her alone in the darkness, with only the sound of the pounding rain to keep her company.

PART II

March 10-20

CHAPTER FIVE

Highway 41,
thirty miles south of Abilene, Texas
Morning of March 10

Harold hadn't counted on such terrible weather.

He'd counted on a lot of things: vaporizations, discontent over the long march, scattered illness, lack of food . . . but not *this*. He wasn't prepared for this.

Crouching by the small rectangular window in back of the slow-moving ambulance, Harold could see about six or seven boys marching right behind him. The rest of the flock was obscured by the sheets of driving rain. The boys' faces were grimly set. Their clothes were soaked. They trudged with the stiffness and determination of soldiers in wartime. And they all looked as if they would gladly rip Harold to shreds.

This is no good. Harold wrung his sweaty palms. *I've got to find a hotel or apartment building or some kind of shelter.*

What was *happening* around here, anyway? The weather was okay when he and his flock of three-hundred-odd kids set out from Austin. Sure, it was raining. But nothing like this. By the time they reached the northern suburbs of the city, they found themselves in the midst of a full-fledged downpour. And it didn't stop.

Now the rain was torrential.

Of course, Harold himself remained perfectly dry. He rode comfortably in the ambulance he'd taken from the hospital—leading the pack, ready to tend to the sick and to distribute food and medical supplies. Larissa accompanied him, along with a promiscuous little brunette named Caroline, who had the most amazing curls and saucer-shaped brown eyes.

It was a nice arrangement. One drove while the other entertained. Together the three of them plodded along at a speed of about five miles per hour: a beacon of flashing lights, a brilliant metaphor for the Ark of the Covenant, the *new* Covenant, where Harold played the role of Moses and these ragtag teenage waifs played the Israelites.

Well. That was the idea, anyway. Harold thought there would be some kind of grand symbolism in the whole thing. He thought the lights and sirens would provide inspiration to his followers. He hadn't thought that they would be caught in a freak monsoon.

No. As it turned out, he'd made a huge mistake. The kids out there were miserable. Utterly miserable. And *pissed*. Why shouldn't they be? They didn't care about *symbolism*. They cared about food and warmth and a dry place to sleep. They should have been at Harold's farm by now. Instead they weren't even halfway there, marching through the worst rain in the history of Texas—

"Harold?" Caroline called from the front.

What? He grimaced. Despite her looks, Caroline had the grating, high-pitched voice of a cartoon character. He would probably have to get rid of her soon. She was the biggest imbecile he'd ever met in his life. Her interests seemed limited to how she missed the Revlon kiosk at the Johnson City Mall. Compared to her, Larissa had the intellectual capacity of Einstein. Couldn't she see he was *thinking,* that he shouldn't be disturbed?

"Well?" he barked.

"Uh . . . well, um, you better come take a look at this."

Finally he tore his gaze from the window and stormed through the cabin—past Larissa, who lay half naked and forgotten on the narrow stretcher. He jammed his head through a tiny porthole into the front of the ambulance, fully intending to yell something obscene in Caroline's ear.

But he didn't.

Uh-oh.

Now he understood what Caroline meant. A group of about thirty boys stood blocking the road.

Harold chewed his lower lip. How did they get in front of him? They must have dropped behind the ambulance until they were out of sight, then ducked into the flat cornfields on either side of the road and sprinted ahead . . . but it didn't matter. He had a serious crisis on his hands. They'd outflanked him. They'd *planned* this. The gravity of the situation was etched into every one of their hard, dripping faces. Caroline slowed to a stop.

"What the hell do they want?" he breathed.

46

"I tried to tell you earlier," Caroline whispered, shaking her head. Her grip remained tight on the steering wheel. "See, I figured something like this was coming. I mean, don't you think this rain is weird, Harold? It's not normal. It's making people crazy. Some of them don't believe in the promised land anymore. I tried to tell them the truth, but they don't want to hear it. A few of 'em came up to me last night and said they wanted the rest of their rations today—"

"Shut up," Harold snapped. He didn't have time for her blather. Besides, there *were* no more rations; he'd barely stocked the ambulance with enough food to feed everyone for one day. He had to think fast. Too bad he'd gone through all the MDMA and Ritalin. He could really use a blast right now.

A few kids began to inch toward the ambulance— very, very slowly.

There were only two viable options, Harold realized. Either he could demand that Caroline step on the gas and mow right through the mob or he could try to talk some sense into them. Neither seemed very promising.

"Doctor Harold!" one of the boys shouted. "Git yer ass out here!"

He swallowed. Now that he thought about it, the first option wouldn't work. He'd need a tank to go through all those kids.

"Come on, Doc!" another one hooted. "Whatcha scared of? I thought you had powers!"

Powers? Fear gnawed at his stomach. It occurred to him that he'd never been *afraid* of these kids before.

Contemptuous, yes. But never afraid. He fought the feeling with every ounce of his strength. He couldn't allow himself to be bullied by a bunch of rednecks—pathetic dolts whom *he* had saved. He was better than they were. Tightening his fists, he withdrew his head from the front and marched back through the ambulance. He'd duped them before, and he would dupe them again. . . .

"What's going on?" Larissa murmured.

Harold didn't answer. There was nothing to say. He tossed open the doors and hopped out of the ambulance.

Damn.

The rain really *was* bad. The drops were so large and fast that they almost *hurt*—plastering his long hair to the sides of his head like a helmet. He blinked, wiping the water from his eyes. The ambulance was surrounded now. There must have been fifty kids out there, and the rest of the flock was rapidly approaching from the rear.

Not all of them were angry, Harold reminded himself. No. Despite their waterlogged misery, some of them still believed in Dr. Harold Wurf. They wouldn't have come this far if they didn't. Harold forced himself to remain collected as he walked around the side to face the crowd in front. A solution *had* to present itself.

"Here comes the Healer," somebody yelled derisively. "I want to see if he can heal himself after we—"

"Enough!" Harold barked. But his voice was hoarse and unconvincing, and nearly drowned out by the rain.

48

The kids began snickering among themselves.

Harold cleared his throat, then climbed onto the hood of the ambulance, pushing himself up with his hands. His jeans were soaked in the process. For a moment, as he tried to stand, he nearly slipped on the slick metal. *Get control!* Finally he managed to plant his feet. *There.* He glared down at the mob through the relentless shower—his face dripping, his breath coming fast. Yes, yes. He was their Moses. He could pull something off.

"Don't you see what's happening here?" he shouted over the storm.

The crowd began to quiet down. Thunder rumbled in the distance.

"It's the Book of Exodus all over again! God is testing us! When Moses led the Israelites through the wilderness, they doubted him at every turn. But God always provided. When they went hungry, he gave them manna!"

He paused, waiting for a response.

Nobody said a word.

Nobody even *reacted*. The same sea of angry and soaking-wet faces stared back at him. Terrific. None of them had a clue what he was talking about. Hadn't any of these losers read the Bible? This was *Texas,* for Christ's sake.

"Hey, Doc," a fat, red-faced boy in overalls growled. "Drop the preacher act and give us some goddamn food, or I'm gonna eat *you.*"

"But I'm—I'm trying to tell you, there . . . there's food ahead," he stammered. He thrust a finger down the highway, struggling to remain self-possessed.

Think. He knew he had to make something up on the spot—just to stall them. "I swear to you that there's food ahead. Shelter, too. Enough for everyone. Right at the next exit off this highway. We'll have all the food and shelter we need."

The fat kid sneered. "You actually expect us to *buy* that crap, Doc?"

"I swear it's true," Harold insisted. He could feel his confidence slipping away.

A few kids laughed.

"I say we just kill him now and *take* the damn food," somebody muttered.

"But there *is* no food!" Harold cried. "That's what I'm trying to tell you! Take a look in the ambulance if you want. We ate it all because I *know* there's food ahead. I've seen a place. In a vision. Only *I* can take you there. Kill me now, and you'll be sure to starve."

There was another pause. Harold shivered, partly from the wetness and partly from alarm. For once nobody—not one soul—was falling for his lies.

"How far is this place, Doc?" the fat kid yelled after a moment.

"Just up the road. The next exit. I swear. Look— I've never lied to you before, right? I've always made good on my promises." The kid just smiled. He had no teeth.

Harold didn't bother to say anything else. What was the point? He was consumed with only one thought: He had to get behind the wheel of this ambulance as quickly as possible. Without a moment's hesitation he jumped off the hood and landed with a wet smack—nearly falling on his face. His knees and ankles burned from the jolt of the impact, but he managed to hobble over to the door and fling it open.

"Move over," he grunted at Caroline.

She gaped at him for an instant, then started squirming across the sopping wet seat. Luckily the engine was still running. He jumped in beside her and yanked the door shut—but a chubby hand prevented it from closing all the way.

Christ!

The fat kid shoved his body between the door and the driver's seat. His beady blue eyes were only inches from Harold's own, shrouded by the pouring rain.

In his other hand he held a dripping six-inch wooden hunting knife with a shiny, pointed blade.

"What do you want?" Harold breathed shakily.

"What do you *think*, Doc?" he replied with a smile. "I wanna dry off. I wanna ride up here with you. I want first dibs on the food. Anyways, if you're telling the truth, you got nothing to worry about, right?"

CHAPTER SIX

**Egyptian Desert,
near El Daheir
Afternoon of March 10**

"The Chosen One . . . is . . . cast adrift. . . ."

There was a flash of lightning, a crack of thunder—and Sarah's moist finger jerked across the yellow parchment. *Dammit!* She'd lost her place again. How did Josh read this thing? Even without any distractions, it was almost impossible to follow the dense jumble of Hebrew letters. The characters were so small and tightly packed. And the light in her bedroom was terrible. Hunching cross-legged on her bed for hours at a time wasn't doing wonders for her posture, either. She would turn into a blind hunchback if she didn't go crazy first—

Stop feeling sorry for yourself! You're gonna get through this!

Clenching her teeth, she determinedly jabbed her finger back onto the scroll. She couldn't let herself get frustrated. She leaned forward and squinted at the same line again, translating the words in her mind as she read right to left: *". . . cast adrift . . . still . . . separated from . . ."*

Ever since she'd wrested the scroll from Ibrahim's thugs, she'd devoted herself to reading it—completely

52

and with undivided attention. She'd conquered her fear out of simple necessity: The scroll represented the only possibility of escape. The *only* possibility. Two armed guards were posted outside her door twenty-four hours a day. She *had* to prove to Ibrahim that the parchment had powers. She had to prove to him that his own fanatical religious beliefs meant nothing—and that it was in everyone's best interest to let her find Josh.

The problem was that she had no idea how to do it. She wasn't even sure if *she* believed in the power of the scroll.

"*. . . separated from . . . her brother,*" she finished. "*The Chosen One is cast adrift, still separated from her brother.*"

She took a deep breath. All right. What was *that* supposed to mean?

It made no sense. The scroll was supposed to include prophecies, right? That's what Josh had said. So it should have talked about something *big,* like the way billions of people had melted. That's what she would have *assumed,* anyway. But almost everything in the scroll was a bunch of weird stuff about the Demon and the Chosen One. And there was no code of any sort—at least as far as she could tell. What had Josh been talking about?

Then again, maybe she was going about this the wrong way. Maybe she was taking the words too *literally.* Could it be that the Chosen One was a symbol or metaphor for something else? Maybe the Chosen One was supposed to personify something—like the way the Grim Reaper personified death. Maybe *that* was the code or the key to the code.

"The Chosen One is cast adrift, still separated from her brother." Okay—so how could that be symbolic? *She'd* been separated from her brother, too. A humorless smile appeared on her lips. Great. If she ever met the Chosen One, they'd have lots to talk about.

Sarah paused for a moment, glancing out the window at the endless rain and darkening evening skies. There was a flash, another crack of thunder. *Jeez.* Talk about depressing. She hadn't seen the sun in weeks. It wasn't *healthy.* It wasn't natural. . . .

No, it wasn't natural at all, was it?

She scowled. Almost three weeks of rain in the desert was downright bizarre, as a matter of fact. Would *that* be in the scroll? Maybe. After all, the Bible talked about rain and floods and natural disasters at the end of the world . . . or something like that. She peered at the parchment again.

"Sarah?" Ibrahim's voice called from the hall.

Get lost, she thought angrily.

"Sarah?"

Maybe if she kept quiet, he would just go away. Her eyes hungrily roved over the next few lines. *Let's see.* . . .

A fist pounded on the door.

"Sarah, it's time to join us for prayer," Ibrahim stated.

She didn't even bother to look up. *Wait a second.* She drew in her breath. There *was* something here: *"Waters will rise—from north to south, from east to west."*

If it rained a lot, then waters would rise. Wouldn't

they? Of course. Ibrahim was always talking about how all the rain was going to flood his estate.

"Come with me now," Ibrahim insisted. "I know you're in there. . . ."

But Sarah had tuned him out. There was something else on the page, too: *The light of the sun will not see the earth.* She blinked a few times, swallowing. Rain certainly prevented the sun from seeing the earth. The words were vague, uncertain . . . but still, they made sense. And all of these phenomena were supposed to occur now: in the Israeli months of Adar and Nisan, 5759—meaning the month of March, 1999.

Right at this very moment.

Blocked sunlight. Rising waters. It's happening, isn't it?

A strange, nervous heat filled Sarah's body. It seemed to spread in ripples from her stomach. She'd never felt a sensation like this before; she couldn't put a name on it. There was excitement, yes . . . but fear, too. Could there *really* be truth to what Elijah claimed about this scroll—that it foretold the future, that it could be used to prevent a terrible calamity?

No. If she were to believe in the prophecies, she *had* to see something more definitive. She kept reading. But there was nothing more about the rain. Just a few lines about the Demon, then a little passage at the bottom that was separated from the main block of text . . .

I know this!

It was that totally bizarre bit that Josh had showed her: *"To be heavenly raises us. Deals make it safer for all fools to read lips. Three twenty-seven ninety-nine."*

Nonsense. Or was it?

"Sarah!" Ibrahim shouted. "The muezzin will call us!"

Ignoring him, she squinted closely at the passage. Josh had mentioned something about these nonsensical asides, the segments that stood alone. He'd brought it to her attention the moment before he was snatched. She racked her brain . . . *Right, right.* He'd said something about how the prophecy was divided according to the twelve lunar cycles of the year except for these parts. *And* that the strange numbers might be connected to the code. But were the numbers also related to the lunar cycles? Her eyes flashed back up to the top of the page.

"In the third lunar cycle, during the months of Adar and Nisan in the year 5759 . . ."

She frowned. The *third* lunar cycle? She hadn't noticed earlier, but that was wrong. Adar and Nisan were the sixth and seventh lunar cycles of the Hebrew calendar. True, they coincided with the third *month* of the Western calendar, but . . .

"I'm coming in," Ibrahim's voice announced.

"Go away!" she finally snapped. Couldn't he take a damn *hint?* She agitatedly shifted on the bed. Now that she remembered, the passage describing the month of Shevat was wrong, too. Shevat was listed as the *second* lunar cycle—even though it was the fifth. Yet it translated as the second *month* of the Western calendar. The strange heat in her body was growing. Could it have been an accident? Unlikely.

As far as she could tell, the scroll revolved around precise months and dates. Such an error would have been unimaginably careless.

Unless . . .

Unless the scroll was written for someone who understands both the Hebrew calendar and the Western calendar. Like me.

The door crashed open.

Ibrahim stood in the archway, swathed in a white cloak and turban. His eyes were blazing. The two guards stood at his side, scimitars drawn.

But Sarah didn't see Ibrahim, or the weapons . . . or anything else in the room. Her mind was far, far away—racing into frightening and unknown territory. The scroll seemed to link the Hebrew calendar and the Western calendar. But that was impossible. The scroll was thousands of years old. It had been written long before the Western calendar was invented or even conceived. So why were the months and dates all mixed up? Her eyes fell back to the parchment, back to the numbers at the bottom of the passage.

"Shalosh essreem v'shevah tisheem v'teyshah."

Three, twenty-seven, ninety-nine.

"It's time to pray!" Ibrahim barked. "Why are you still in bed?"

Sarah gasped. If the scroll *were* geared toward somebody who understood the Western calendar, then those three numbers could easily represent a date. An *exact* date. She shook her head, trembling. It would make perfect sense: This passage was about the month of March. The third month. In the year 1999. *3/27/99.* The longer she stared at the numbers, the more certain

57

she became of their meaning. What *else* could they mean?

My God.

Her heart was pounding now. If 3/27/99 truly was a date . . . then Elijah was right. He was *right*. All his wild beliefs, everything she'd derided in the past—all of it was true. And if that were the case . . .

Sarah chewed her lip. Until this moment she'd never believed in anything mystical, anything unseen. But then again, until this moment she'd never had proof.

There *was* something powerful and supernatural hidden in the scroll.

Because whoever had inscribed this parchment thousands of years ago had somehow foreseen a different way of measuring time. The numbers *proved* it. Whoever had written these prophecies had looked into the future—knowing that someone like Elijah or Josh or Sarah would read the numbers and understand their meaning in the context of the present time.

It's the first step, she realized. *The first step* . . .

"Sarah!" Ibrahim was shouting. "Sarah! Why aren't you listening to me?"

An electric feeling surged through her. She found she was terrified and elated all at once. Ibrahim would *have* to believe in the scroll now—because *she* believed in it. The coincidences were simply too unlikely; the scroll's power had to be authentic. Any lingering doubt faded from her mind. She jumped from the bed and dashed across the room.

"Come here!" she yelled, grasping Ibrahim's wrist. She tried to yank him toward the bed.

But Ibrahim wouldn't budge. "What *is* it?" he demanded.

"You gotta look at this," she answered breathlessly. "I've cracked the first part of the code. I can prove it."

His face darkened. "The *code?*"

She kept tugging at him—but he stood perfectly immobile, like a statue. Finally she let go. "Just *look* at this!" she cried, waving her hand at the parchment spread on the mattress. "I can prove to you that this scroll has power. I mean, I can prove to you that the person who *wrote* it has power. I don't know what kind exactly, I just know it—"

"Sarah, please," Ibrahim cut in. He folded his arms across his chest. "Enough."

In frustration she ran to the bed and gingerly grasped the scroll's wooden handles, then spread it on the floor at his feet. "Just listen to me," she panted, dropping to her knees. She stabbed her hand at the text. "There's a date right here: March 27, 1999. How would somebody in ancient Israel know about a date in the modern calendar?"

He gazed at her a moment, then sighed and shook his head. "Sarah, do you realize that you sound like a madwoman?"

"*Me?*" she cried. "What about *you?* Is what I'm saying any crazier than that stuff about the hidden Imam and the End of Days and—"

"Be quiet!" he barked. "I will hear no more blasphemy!" He snapped his fingers twice.

Uh-oh. Sarah knew what *that* meant: The guards were being summoned. In a panic she reached for the

59

scroll's handles—and found the blade of a scimitar at her neck.

"Wait!" she gasped. "Don't . . ."

But the sharp, cold metal pressed into her skin, silencing her. The force of it wasn't enough to puncture the flesh or draw blood; it was just enough to cause some discomfort—a hint of the *real* pain it could deliver. She remained paralyzed, watching helplessly as the other guard gathered the scroll into his arms.

The color drained from her face.

"I'm confiscating that *junk,*" Ibrahim stated disdainfully. "You may have it back, but only after you have proven that you can be responsible. That means you will start coming to prayer with us instead of hiding in your room like a child. Am I making myself understood?"

She could only muster a feeble whimper as the guard hurried from the room with the scroll. "But you have to believe me," she croaked. "I can prove it."

Ibrahim chuckled softly. "What can you prove to me, Sarah? You know I don't read Hebrew. Suppose I showed *you* some old Arabic scroll. What would prevent me from making all kinds of outrageous claims about *that?*"

"You think I'm *lying?*" she shrieked, forgetting the blade at her neck.

Ibrahim shrugged. "Allah is testing me." He shot a quick glance at the guard behind her, then nodded. The guard withdrew the sword. "I don't pretend to understand His ways. . . ."

But Sarah wouldn't hear the rest of it. Seizing the

moment, she lunged forward and scrambled out the door.

"Come back here!" she screamed after the second guard. "Give me—"

She abruptly fell silent.

The narrow corridor was empty.

She spun in horror—first to the right, then to the left. The guard had vanished. A dozen doors lined the walls on either side; he could have escaped into any one of them. This place was a labyrinth. She'd never find him.

The scroll was gone.

SEVEN

Highway 41,
twenty miles south of Abilene, Texas
Afternoon of March 10

"So where *is* this magical food supply, Doc?" the fat boy asked. "I'm starved."

Harold checked his side mirrors again. He didn't need to do it; the ambulance rolled along the flat highway at a sluggish crawl—and there was no traffic. But the gesture was symbolic. He was refusing to acknowledge the fat kid's presence. Acknowledging him would be a sign of weakness. And even though the kid had stuffed himself between Harold and Caroline like an oversized Christmas ham, Harold maintained perfect driving-instructor form: back straight, hands on the wheel at two and ten o'clock, windshield wipers and headlights adjusted for the pouring rain.

It was an act, of course.

In truth, Harold was playing out a dozen different escape scenarios in his mind. And he was getting worried. Nothing seemed feasible. The kid still clutched the knife in his left hand. He could plunge the blade into Harold's chest before Harold even reached for the door.

At the very least, however, Harold had been lucky in terms of buying himself some more time. Extraordinarily lucky, in fact. He'd passed three exits in the past hour, and each had been blocked with the rusted heaps of cars whose drivers had most likely vaporized. But that luck would eventually run out. The laws of probability weren't that kind. Sooner or later an exit would be clear, and Harold would have to make a move.

"Better slow down there," the fat boy growled. He glanced in the rearview mirror. "You don't wanna lose any of our buddies, do ya?"

Of course I do, Harold thought, but he eased up on the gas. He'd been nudging up the speed with each passing mile. He wanted to sneak as much distance as possible between himself and the people on foot—in case he had to make a desperate break for it. He'd assumed that this kid had been paying much more attention to Caroline than the speedometer. After all, the kid was practically slobbering over her, with his fleshy right arm draped around her shoulders.

"I'm talkin' to you, Doc," the kid stated. *Ahm tawkin' tuh yew.* "You don't wanna lose any of your precious followers. Right?"

Harold could feel the kid's eyes on him now. His arms tensed. He stared at the road.

"Would you *mind?*" Caroline suddenly snapped.

She tried to squirm out from under the kid's arm, but there wasn't enough room to maneuver in the cramped front seat. In the commotion the kid's huge elbow slammed into the right side of Harold's head. Harold jerked at the pain—and the ambulance swerved for a moment. Its slow-moving tires squealed faintly on the wet pavement.

"Yee-haw!" the kid cried. He giggled, then slapped Harold's knee with the flat edge of his knife. "Sorry 'bout that, Doc! Didn't mean to scare ya!"

"What the hell is your problem?" Caroline yelled. "Do you want to get us all killed? Can't you understand that Harold is trying to save your life? Are you that stupid?"

The kid giggled again. "Aww, c'mon, sugar. I'm just tryin' to have some fun. What's your name, anyways? Huh, princess? Mine's Duane."

Duane, Harold thought scornfully. *I should have guessed.* Rage simmered in his veins. He gripped the steering wheel so tightly that his knuckles cracked. His skull was throbbing; his thigh burned from the slap. Yet self-control prevented him from uttering so much as a peep. He wouldn't say a word. Fools like Duane needed constant stimulation. Silence would make him nervous. It was textbook psychology: Nervousness eventually led to anger, which led to carelessness. And then Duane might make a mistake that Harold could exploit.

"Listen up, honey," Duane said after a minute. "You and me both know the Doc here is full of it. He ain't even a real doctor. I say we dump him on the side of the road. Then we go find someplace where we can be alone. Huh? How's that sound?"

Caroline snorted. "You make me sick."

"Sick?" Duane cried. "Sick? Baby—you gotta give me a chance. You don't even know how good it can get till you get it from Duane."

Harold tuned out the conversation, partially for sanity's sake and partially because the landscape ahead was changing. The flat cornfields were coming to an end, giving way to trees and rolling hills. He bit his lip.

64

There was something else, too . . . barely visible in the mist and rain. Something man-made.

No, not yet. Please . . .

But he could see it clearly now: the unmistakable green rectangle of an exit sign—posted at the right side of the road, maybe five hundred yards away.

" . . . so is this it, Doc?" Duane was asking. "Huh? Is this the place?"

Oh, God. A sickening emptiness filled Harold's stomach. As the ambulance drew closer the sign's white block letters swam into view: Exit 13: Cross Plains. 1/4 Mile.

"Well, Doc?" Duane demanded. His voice was clipped. "Is *this* the place?"

The ambulance continued to glide inexorably toward the sign . . . nearer, nearer, then past it. They were close now. Very close. And all evidence seemed to indicate that Harold's luck had indeed run out. No wreckage blocked the spot where the exit road veered off from the highway. He licked his dry lips.

"I'm asking you a question," Duane snarled. *Ahm axin' yew uh question.*

For the first time all afternoon Harold glanced directly into Duane's pudgy red face. It was twisted in a look of utter reprehension. His eyes flashed to Caroline. She didn't look so happy, either. Her smooth and sexy dark features were creased with worry.

"Answer me!" Duane barked. "Is this the place?"

Harold turned back to the road. He had to say yes. It was obvious to everyone in the car that the exit was unobstructed. He couldn't maintain the illusion any longer.

"Yes, Duane," he finally answered. "This is the place. Just like I told you."

Out of the corner of his eye he saw Duane smile. The boy had the creamy smile of a sadist, of a miserable loser who had probably waited his entire life to inflict pain on somebody handsome and gifted like Harold. . . .

I can't believe it. After all I've achieved, this is how I'm going to die.

Harold shook his head. The whole situation was absurdly cliché. How many B movies ended the same way—with a poor sociopath wreaking violence on a charismatic hero? How many dime-store novels featured similar climaxes? It was so ridiculous. . . .

"What're *you* smilin' about?" Duane demanded.

Nothing you could possibly understand, Harold silently replied. With a tired sigh he steered the car off the highway. The road curved off to the right, cut through some trees, then reached another broad thoroughfare. Blank traffic lights swayed in the rain, hanging from wires above the intersection. The tangled, rust-covered ruins of a bus and three cars lay among piles of clothes and huge puddles on the pavement. It looked like a thousand other dead places they'd seen along the way. Harold slowed to a stop.

"You want to know why he's smiling?" Caroline cried excitedly. "He's smiling because he's going to feed his flock! We're almost there!"

Jesus. Harold nearly laughed. At least *somebody* still believed him. But her squeaky optimism was pretty comical in the face of their bleak surroundings. Did she really see any promise of food around here?

"We're almost there, huh?" Duane asked. His voice took on a gruff edge. "Which way?"

Harold stole a quick peek at Duane's lap. The knife lay there; Duane's fingers stroked the wooden handle. Harold quickly scanned the intersection for some kind of sign, *anything* that could postpone the inevitable—but it was hopeless. He caught a glimpse of the rest of the flock in the rearview mirror, approaching from the rear. He was going to have to improvise.

"Which *way*, Doc?" Duane repeated.

Holding his breath, Harold slammed his foot on the gas pedal. The ambulance screeched forward. His head was instantly thrown against the seat.

"What the hell are you *doing?*" Duane shouted. "Goddammit . . ."

But Harold furiously spun the wheel to the right, clawing at it hand over hand. Duane slammed against him. The ambulance tilted up on its two left tires, sandwiching Harold's body between Duane and the door. *The pain!* Harold saw Duane swipe at him with the knife, but the force of the turn sent Duane's fist crashing into the window.

"Ow!" Duane cried.

The knife fell from his grasp, dropping between the seat and the door.

Without pausing for breath Harold spun the wheel in the opposite direction. The ambulance tumbled back onto all four tires, bouncing violently, and Duane fell off him. But Harold was no longer in control. He desperately jabbed at the brakes with his foot. He found himself kicking at an empty space. His body was thrown too far to the left. He tried to compensate by stomping blindly to the right—and wound up hitting the gas again.

"Help me!" Caroline screamed. "Help . . ."

But Harold was powerless. The ambulance careened wildly down the road at a skewed angle. It was headed straight for some scrub brush. *Where are the damn brakes?*

Seconds later the ambulance hurtled into the wall of twigs and leaves. Harold could do nothing but stare. The seat shuddered; Harold and Duane knocked skulls . . . and then they were still.

Pent-up air exploded from Harold's lungs.

The front seat was very quiet—except for the sound of pattering rain and Caroline's soft weeping. It took Harold a few seconds to realize that the right side of the ambulance had been pushed up in the air. Everyone was leaning to the left. But there was no time to waste. He had to get out. He struggled to extricate his arm from between his body and the door frame. It was nearly impossible; he had to contend with the weight of Duane's body as well as his own. With a savage pull he finally freed his left hand. Then he grasped the door handle and squeezed.

The door fell open, and Harold toppled into the rain-soaked mud.

Duane collapsed on top of him.

"Oof," Harold groaned. He shoved Duane into a puddle and staggered to his feet. He had no strategy, no plan of action—other than to hightail it for the woods as fast as possible. . . .

Then he froze. *Uh-oh.*

Dozens of kids were tearing at him through the storm, their faces hideous masks of vengeance and ecstasy. Harold's legs seemed to turn to liquid.

They want to kill me, he realized, petrified. *They want to—*

But the kids swept right past him.

What the . . .

He whirled to see where they were headed—and his jaw dropped.

Not fifty yards past the wrecked ambulance, through a clearing in the brush, was a recreational vehicle. No, *several* recreational vehicles. Lying in the mud. And a collection of trailers, too. His eyes bulged. A few yards beyond the trailers, behind some trees, was the back end of a green truck. Its doors were emblazoned with the words *Fig Newtons.*

Cookies?

"The Healer has shown us the way!" Larissa yelled, scampering past him.

"He spoke the truth!" another girl cried. "Truth!"

For once in his life Harold failed to comprehend the situation. Was this real? Stumbling upon a truckload of cookies was more than fortuitous; it defied imagination. Not even *he* had that kind of luck. He shook his head, watching as the unruly horde swarmed upon the truck, tearing open its doors. A wild cheer erupted, and a shower of plastic containers exploded into the rain.

"Son of a bitch," somebody muttered next to him. "Nobody's *this* damn lucky."

Duane. In his stupor Harold had almost forgotten about him. But the grudging complaint was enough to snap Harold back into focus.

He *was* this lucky. Of course he was. He was Dr. Harold Wurf. Sweet relief surged through his bruised and battered frame. This was real. He'd been saved. Saved! The way he *always* had. . . . It was another sign of his power. He turned to look into the fat jerk's beady little eyes.

"I think a 'thank you' would be more appropriate," Harold said smugly.

"Go screw yourself," Duane replied. He spat on the mud at Harold's feet, then limped off toward the Fig Newtons truck, where most of the kids were already stuffing their faces.

Harold frowned. *Idiot,* he thought. But Duane's words made him think. Even the afterglow of *this* sudden miracle wouldn't last. People would thank him now, but the triumph would fade. Then fools like Duane would start trouble. They hated Harold for his luck and knowledge—and their hatred kept growing. He would have to deal with them eventually.

"I knew you'd feed us!" Caroline cried, shattering his thoughts. "I knew it!"

He glanced over his shoulder. She was eagerly squirming out of the ambulance into the rain. Once again she wore that wonderful look of pure adoration.

At least he had *her.* Larissa, too. They would do anything for him. *Anything.*

Yes. Water pounded on his skull, but the well-oiled cogs in his brain whirred and hummed. There was no limit to what Caroline and Larissa would do, was there? So if the two of them performed a few choice little tasks, he could probably deal with Duane and the other nonbelievers. Yes, yes. It would be wise to act *soon*, too—while the victory was still fresh and the flock was content. He could strike a preemptive blow.

Then he'd never have to rely on fate or good fortune again.

Bethany,
Illinois
Night of March 14

Something strange is happening to me.
I can't put my finger on it. I know it
doesn't have anything to do with the
visions because I don't seem to have
them anymore. I haven't had them since
we left Jackson. I don't feel the need
to go west, either. It doesn't make
any sense.

The thing is, when the visions used to
come, I could point to them and say
that they affected me. I couldn't say
how exactly. I couldn't explain them in
any way. I just know that they were
there. I know they were real.

But this feeling is a lot more subtle.
And the weird thing is, it feels good.

That's the big difference. I'm not used to that!

I still keep asking myself every day: Am I going nuts? Am I losing my mind? But this time it's not because I'm scared. No. Ever since George and I found this abandoned cabin out here on Lake Shelbyville, I find myself smiling a lot. And laughing. And forgetting about all the horrible things that have happened to the planet, and the people I love, and everything else. Even those insane girls from Jackson seem like a distant memory.

Maybe that is crazy. I'm not sure. All I know is that I don't really want the feeling to end. For once, at least some of the time, I'm happy.

But I guess I shouldn't worry about it. I should just enjoy it, right?

I think part of the feeling could have to do with where I am. Sleeping in a huge bed in a cozy log cabin every *night, right next to a roaring fire, right next to a beautiful lake, listening to the raindrops and thunder . . . it's easy to forget about problems. I never realized how much I love the outdoors.*

I don't even mind the rain anymore.

Julia glanced over the page in the crackling firelight. She figured she'd written enough for one evening. After a long sigh she closed the frayed notebook and tossed it aside, then spread out across the huge bed that filled most of the one-room cabin.

It was so nice to be able to write *freely*—without worrying that somebody was looking over her shoulder, invading her privacy, trying to steal her secrets. Luke had always hated it when she wrote in her diary. But George never bothered her about it. He kept to himself at those times, preferring to sit by the stone fireplace or on a stool in the tiny kitchenette. He *respected* her.

I could get used to living like this, she thought.

"Are you all done?"

George's voice drifted from somewhere across the room. Julia sat up straight. For a moment she couldn't locate him. He wasn't in his usual spot in front of the fire. She glanced around—then saw his hunched frame in a dark corner by the small refrigerator. "What are you doing over there?" she asked with a puzzled grin.

He shrugged. "I . . . uh, just wanted to let you

have your space," he mumbled. His hands were stuffed in the pockets of his grubby jeans. He stared at the tops of his black Dr. Martens, looking sheepish and uncomfortable. "I didn't want to bother you or anything."

"*Bother* me?" She laughed. "Come on, you couldn't bother me if you tried. My space is your space." She propped herself up on the pillows and slapped the bedspread. "Come here. I'm sorry. I don't mean to put you off when I write."

George slowly stepped out of the shadows, but he paused at the foot of the bed. He kept his head down. Julia cocked an eyebrow. What was going on? He usually wasn't *this* shy. *Hold on* . . . Was he blushing? His face seemed flushed. Maybe it was the light of the fire.

"Hey, what is it?" she asked. "What's wrong?"

He glanced up at her, then quickly glanced back down. His stringy blond bangs flopped in front of his face. "Nothing," he said. She could tell by the sound of his voice that he was smiling. "It's just that—um, you're not wearing any pants."

She glanced down at herself. *Oops.* She hadn't even realized it—but she'd been lounging around in nothing but a T-shirt and a pair of bikini underwear.

Now *she* was blushing.

But she had a perfectly good reason for going seminaked: Her jeans were soaked from the rain, so they were drying by the fire. Besides, she felt so comfortable around George that she hadn't given her clothing a second thought.

75

"I can put some on if you like," she offered. "I don't want to make you uncomfortable or anything. It's just that my pants are wet—"

"No, no," George interrupted. He laughed nervously. "I mean, do whatever you want. I, uh . . . you know, I don't care either way."

She couldn't help but grin again. Did he *want* her to walk around in her underwear? After all, he was a sixteen-year-old boy. But her legs were so sticklike and ugly. Then again, *any* pair of female legs would probably look nice to a sixteen-year-old boy.

"What are you thinking?" George asked in the silence.

She shrugged. "I was just thinking that . . ." Her voice trailed off. She was going to make up something, but what was the point? George could handle the truth. He probably knew what she was thinking, anyway. He always did.

She took a deep breath. "I'm flattered that you were looking at my legs, actually. If you really want to know, I don't think I'm very pretty."

He frowned. *"You?* You're gorgeous. I mean—" He quickly shut his mouth. He started staring at his feet again. "Forget it," he mumbled.

Gorgeous? Nobody had *ever* called her gorgeous before. Luke used to call her Ugly as a pet name.

"Thanks, George," she whispered. "That—"

"Hey, you know what?" he interrupted in a loud voice. "I haven't had any blackouts or flashes recently. Not since we left Jackson."

Poor George. All this talk about their appearances was making him nervous.

"Neither have I," she said after a moment. "And I haven't been thinking about going west that much."

"Me neither." He sat down at the foot of the bed, but he kept his eyes averted. He stared at an imaginary spot on the bedspread. "What do you think it is? Why would the visions stop?"

Julia shrugged. "Dunno. It's kind of nice, though, isn't it?"

"I guess," he said uncertainly. "But I think all that stuff is important, don't you? I mean, ever since New Year's all I could think of was moving west, finding the Chosen One. And now it's just gone. It doesn't feel right."

She nodded. "Yeah. But we'll be on the road again soon. As soon as the rain lets up . . ."

"And our food runs out," they finished simultaneously.

"Hey!" George exclaimed. A smile crossed his face. "Have you noticed that? We're always saying the exact same thing at the same time?"

"Nooo," she teased. "You think so?"

He started laughing. Julia laughed, too. She couldn't help it. When he was happy like that, when he totally forgot himself and gave in to the moment, he looked just like a little kid. His entire face seemed to come alive.

"Anybody ever tell you you've got a cute smile?" she asked.

His head jerked up. "What?" He looked stricken—as if she had accused him of a crime.

She giggled. "It's a *compliment*, George."

He blinked a few times, then managed a weak

77

grin. "Yeah, yeah. I mean . . . thanks." His eyes fell back to the bedspread. He laughed once. "You think most people are like you and me? You think most people think they look like crap?"

Julia raised her eyebrows. "Are you kidding? Luke thought he was God's gift to the world. He always talked about 'breaking into the modeling thing'—like he even had a chance."

At the mention of Luke's name George's face soured slightly. Julia suddenly wished she hadn't brought up her ex-boyfriend. It had been a reflex, a natural response after years of repressed hostility. *Never again,* she resolved. She had to work on driving Luke from her mind—for good.

"You still think about Luke a lot?" George asked after a moment. He glanced up at her.

"More than I'd like," she admitted.

George nodded. His bright green eyes seemed to lose some of their sparkle. "Yeah, I guess I can understand that," he mumbled. His voice sounded funny, as if there were something caught in his throat. "You guys were together a long time. I mean, it's natural that you would still feel something for him."

"I don't, George," she stated. "I don't feel anything for him."

He stared at her. He chewed his lip, as if he were frightened by what he was going to say. "I'm glad," he finally breathed. His voice was thick. "Because—uh, because it would really bum me out if you did."

Julia found herself staring back at him. *It would?* His words struck a curious chord inside her. She didn't want to make George upset . . . and sitting here with him by the light of the fire, she discovered she couldn't even conjure up Luke's face.

And in that instant things became clear.

She began to understand why she was so happy. The reason had been right in front of her all along, but it had been so far-fetched, so impossible . . . yet so obvious at the same time. She hadn't been able to give her happiness a name until now.

George.

Her hand reached out and caressed his cheek, seemingly of its own volition.

George didn't move. His body was trembling.

"What's wrong?" she whispered.

His gaze was unblinking, his breathing steady. "I . . ." He swallowed. "I just don't want to mess things up."

Mess things up? Her heart seemed to squeeze; it was the sweetest thing anyone had ever said to her. It was *perfect*. She leaned toward him across the soft mattress. "You could never mess things up," she breathed.

Their faces drew closer.

"Never?" he asked.

"No." And before he could ask another question, she planted a soft kiss on his lips.

CHAPTER NINE

**Egyptian Desert,
near El Daheir
Night of March 15**

Sarah drummed her freshly painted fingernails along the end of the long, lacquered oak dinner table. Where was Ibrahim? She'd been waiting for over ten minutes—and *she'd* been late. She'd been hoping to make a dramatic entrance. Her plan was to shock Ibrahim with the devastating beauty of her dress: a sleeveless black evening gown she found in a walk-in closet near her bedroom.

Well, that was *part* of her plan, anyway.

Now she was starting to get anxious. The cavernous dining room tended to make her a little uneasy, anyway; it was much too opulent for her taste—with its vaulted ceiling and candelabra and hanging tapestries. She always felt if she were dining at the White House or Buckingham Palace. It was *especially* nerve-racking when the only other people present were the two silent, stone-faced guards by the door. They wouldn't so much as glance at her. But for the past five days she'd been playing along with the stiff formality of mealtimes. And that wasn't all. She did anything she could to please Ibrahim . . . matching his flawless manners, smiling politely at his boring conversation, looking him straight in the eye when he told her that he loved her. She'd even begun to study an English translation of the Koran: the sacred text of Islam. And when it came time to pray in the direction of Mecca, she dutifully knelt beside him, five times a day. Most impressively, she hadn't mentioned the scroll once.

She had a simple reason. She wanted to convince Ibrahim that *she* was falling in love with *him*. Because once that happened, his defenses would drop.

Then she would steal the scroll. Then she would get back to Jerusalem and find Josh.

She didn't want to think about how far-fetched or impossible that scenario might be. She clung to the plan with the fervor of a zealot. It was all she had.

Sarah knew she wasn't much of an actress. She'd *never* been able to act. From what she could tell, acting was basically a glorified form of lying—and she was a lousy liar. It wasn't a fluke that she'd wanted to be a journalist; it would have been the perfect career. She would have spent her entire life sifting through lies and reporting the truth. . . .

But there was no point in dwelling on the past. Ibrahim wouldn't *accept* the truth. Besides, the past meant nothing now, not after what she'd learned about the scroll. Somewhere in that parchment was the key to her survival, to the survival of everyone on the planet. So she had to deceive Ibrahim. She had to lull him into thinking he could trust her. Trust was the key. If he trusted her, he would reveal where the scroll was hidden.

I have to make him believe in me.

There was a clatter of footsteps outside the door.

Sarah took a deep breath and brushed aside a strand of her long brown hair. Her nose twitched. She wasn't wearing her glasses. She *was* wearing makeup, however—eyeliner, ruby lipstick, and blush. All the gunk made her face feel dirty; she hadn't worn makeup in years. But it was like a mask. The changes were part of a costume. She was playing a role tonight. And in a way the fantasy of it kept her from facing the unthinkable reality of what she planned to do.

This is it. Show time.

"Sarah, I'm so sorry I'm late," Ibrahim apologized as he strode into the room. He slumped into the chair beside her. "Forgive me. I've . . . I've had a difficult day."

She stared at him. Something was very wrong. His short black hair stood in damp disarray. He'd obviously just come from outside because his cloak was wet. His riding boots had tracked mud across the pristine stone floor. He *always* changed before dinner. Always.

"What happened?" she murmured.

He sighed, rubbing his face with his hands. "Nawaf . . . do you remember Nawaf?"

She shook her head, bewildered.

"He's my stable boy," he said. He let his hands flop to his lap. Dark circles ringed his normally bright eyes. "That is to say, he *was* my stable boy. He was also far more than that." His voice grew strained. "He was my dear friend. I—I'm sure I introduced you to him."

"Ibrahim, what happened?" she repeated. "What's wrong?"

Ibrahim glanced up at her. "He—he vaporized," he stuttered. "We were out riding by the edge of the estate.

He called to me . . . and then he disappeared into one of those awful black puddles. It was over in a flash." A tear fell from his cheek. He furiously wiped at his eyes. "The horse kept going. It took off into the rain. . . ."

"I'm so sorry," she whispered. She leaned toward him and touched his arm.

Ibrahim could only shake his head. He slouched forward, sobbing.

Impulsively Sarah pushed herself out of her velvety chair. She stood behind him, gently massaging his broad shoulders.

Oh, my God. What am I doing?

Several moments passed before she realized she was *comforting* the man she hated. But she couldn't help it; her sympathy was genuine. She *did* feel sorry for him.

But that was good, wasn't it? Yes . . . as a matter of fact, it was better than anything she could have planned. She wasn't lying. She could lose herself in these emotions to get what she wanted. It was an act, to be sure—but it was a *real* one. Ibrahim was at his most vulnerable right now. And when people were vulnerable, they were more likely to seek solace in somebody they loved. They were more easily manipulated.

"I'm sorry, Sarah," he mumbled. He cleared his throat and straightened up. "I don't mean to carry on like this. We should eat."

But Sarah kept kneading the tense muscles around his neck. "No, it's good to carry on," she whispered. "It's good to let your emotions go."

He glanced up at her. "B-but aren't you hungry?" he stammered.

She shook her head. "No. Are you?"

"I suppose not. Still—" He broke off, his moist eyes narrowing. "My goodness," he breathed. "You look stunning."

I was hoping you'd say that, she thought. She shrugged modestly. Her fingers wandered down his back. . . . She began to probe the taut, sinewy spot under his shoulder blades.

"I just wanted to look nice for you tonight," she murmured. "Is that okay?"

His mouth hung slack. "Sarah, what's gotten into you?" he finally asked.

"Nothing," she answered. Her tone was breezy and nonchalant. She focused all her energy on maintaining a steady gaze. These next few moments were going to be difficult; she knew that she had to be honest whenever possible. "I guess I'm just in a funny mood. I've been doing a lot of thinking in these past few days."

He swallowed. "About what?"

"About us, Ibrahim." And that was true. She *had* been thinking about the two of them. She'd just been thinking about how she could trick him.

"What about . . . *us?*" he asked cautiously.

Sarah cast a furtive glance at the guards, then brought her lips to his ear. "Can we go someplace where we can talk alone? I don't feel so comfortable here."

"Well, I . . . yes, yes." He quickly pushed himself from the table.

She stood right next to him, very close—closer than what she would normally accept as a comfortable distance between two people.

84

Ibrahim blinked. Then he shuffled toward the door with his head down. Sarah matched him step for step. He was clearly troubled by her behavior. He kept looking at her and looking away, agitated and distracted. *Good.* She was making him nervous. She was gaining control.

"We'll go to my room," he mumbled as they passed between the two guards. They stepped into a large foyer dominated by a sweeping spiral staircase.

The guards remained in place—like suits of armor on display. Sarah breathed a secret sigh of relief. They weren't following. She and Ibrahim were alone.

"I'm glad you want to talk," Ibrahim said. "I need some companionship tonight. And the fact that it's you, the woman I love . . . I can't tell you how happy that makes me."

Here I go, she thought. Her heart fluttered. *The performance of a lifetime.*

Without a word she slipped her hand into his, letting their fingers intertwine as they slowly climbed the stairs. Only then did she allow herself to face the deed that awaited her.

In a matter of minutes she was going to seduce this man. This virtual *stranger.*

She was going to throw herself at him, coax him into bed, surrender her virginity in a charade of passion. *Her.* Sarah Levy—a girl who had kissed only three boys in her entire lifetime. True, none of them was anywhere *near* as good-looking as Ibrahim . . . but still, she'd kissed them all willingly.

Yet was this act *unwilling?* She couldn't even say. She hated Ibrahim, but she *had* to seduce him to get

85

the scroll. There was something loathsome and thrilling and terrifying about it all at once. Losing your virginity was a defining event in life—if not *the* defining event. It wasn't as if she'd never thought about it. But now she didn't know what she felt or what she was *supposed* to feel . . . other than a stream of intense physical sensations: dry mouth, dizziness, and shortness of breath.

Thankfully Ibrahim didn't notice. He seemed to be lost in his own world, too. His face was an inscrutable mask as they reached the second floor.

It *was* an undeniably gorgeous mask, though, wasn't it?

Maybe that shouldn't make a difference . . . but it did. And she couldn't pretend it didn't.

"What are you thinking, Sarah?"

She jerked up her head. She hadn't noticed, but they had reached the end of the long hall. They were right outside his door. Her face instantly reddened. "I, uh . . ."

"You don't want to come in?" he asked, gazing at her apprehensively.

"No, no, of course I do," she stammered. "Please, I want to."

He smiled. "Very well." He pushed open the door, then stepped aside to allow her to enter first.

For a few seconds, as she stepped across the threshold, she was overwhelmed by the sheer magnificence of the place. She'd never been to his bedroom before. It must have been four times the size of *her* room—furnished with the most beautiful set of ebony dressers, desks, chairs, and bureaus she'd ever seen. It reminded her of a furniture showroom. The round, tapestry-strewn bed was big enough to sleep a hundred people. She whirled to face him, speechless.

He closed the door and smiled. "Welcome," he said.

Say something! she ordered herself.

But she couldn't. She could only stare into his eyes. . . .

All at once she rushed over to him and passionately forced her lips against his.

"Mrggmf!" He shoved his hands against her shoulders. "Sarah, *please!*"

She blinked in surprise. "What?" she asked. "What's the matter?"

"What's the matter?" he cried. He wriggled away from her and stumbled back against the door. "You're trying to kiss me!"

"I—I know," she stammered uncomprehendingly. She felt very hot all of a sudden. "I mean, I didn't—"

"We can't kiss yet!" he interrupted. "It's not . . . it's not proper!"

Proper? Her eyes narrowed.

"I'm sorry, I'm sorry," he muttered. He began pacing across the room, rubbing his hands together, shaking his head. "I know . . . I mean I know you American girls are very sophisticated. But here, in my country, in my *tradition,* things are done differently. We must wait until we are officially wed. . . ."

An embarrassed smile crept across her face. She couldn't believe it. Not once did she consider that *he* would refuse *her* advances. It was ridiculous: *She* was practically the biggest prude she knew. But *he* was bigger! Talk about humiliating . . .

". . . hope you understand," he rambled on. "It's not that I'm not honored by your—"

"Ibrahim, it's *fine*," she interrupted. She glanced awkwardly around the room, avoiding his eyes. She just wanted to leave as quickly as possible. "*I'm* the one who should apologize."

He slumped into a desk chair and buried his face in his hands. "This is a terrible misunderstanding."

But Sarah wasn't paying attention.

Something had caught her eye. Poking out from under the desk, right next to his muddy riding boots, were the tips of two battered wooden pegs.

Familiar wooden pegs.

The scroll!

She quickly shifted her gaze back to Ibrahim.

"You know what?" she blurted. "I think I better go."

"Yes," he mumbled. He was still rubbing his face. "I think that would be wise—"

"I'll see you in the morning. I'm really, really sorry."

She hurried out the door and slammed it behind her. *Yes!* She *found* it! Okay, she probably shouldn't try anything today; she didn't want to arouse suspicion after that little disaster. But she knew where the scroll was—and that it was safe. Somehow she'd pulled it off. She didn't even have to compromise her sexual status. Judging from Ibrahim's views on chastity, it looked as though she never would. At this point her escape was inevitable.

All she needed was a plan.

CHAPTER
TEN

**Cross Plains Trailer Park,
near Abilene, Texas
Night of March 18**

"Help me," the girl whispered. She lay on the stained linoleum floor of the trailer, clutching her stomach, her eyes rolling. "Please, help me, Doctor. . . ."

I'm trying, goddammit.

Harold was out of patience. He knelt beside the girl and pressed two fingers against the artery in her neck. Her pulse was rapid, faint, erratic. Under the sickly glare of fluorescent lights her skin appeared to be a kind of translucent green. Rancid sweat covered her body, filling the tiny room with a suffocating stench. She didn't have much time—and there wasn't a damn thing he could do about it. Besides, there was somewhere else he needed to be. . . .

"Can't you save her, Dr. Harold?" her boyfriend kept pestering from the doorway. "Can't you do something—"

"Shut up!" Harold snapped. The guy was such a whiny, sniveling little wimp. "Look—just get out of here, all right? Wait outside. I'll let you know."

The boy hesitated. "Wait outside? But the rain—"

"Get out!" Harold barked. He waved his hand impatiently, keeping his eyes fixed on the girl's heaving chest.

89

A moment later the door slammed.

Whew. Finally. Did that guy really want to be in here when his girlfriend croaked? She had acute food poisoning. It wasn't a pretty way to go. Nausea, vomiting, delirium, death. Ba-da-bing, ba-da-boom. Harold had already seen seventeen other cases like this one in the past few days. He *told* those kids not to eat any of that meat they found in the refrigerators of the waterlogged trailers and RVs. It was too old, unfit for consumption.

But did they listen? No. Of course not.

Hey, if the kids *wanted* to get sick, fine. They just shouldn't come running to Harold anymore. Most of his medical supplies had been destroyed or spoiled in this freakish, unending storm. The kids *knew* that. The wrecked ambulance was flooded. All he had left were some pills—opiates mostly. None of them could possibly help in a case like this except to dull the pain. He needed a stomach pump, for God's sake. He needed a life-support machine.

Above all, however, he needed to get out of *here*.

Tonight marked the first crucial step in his plan to deal with the nonbelievers. He was supposed to meet Caroline and Larissa at a secluded spot in the woods. He had to find out how their respective evenings had gone. They were probably already waiting in the rain. . . .

Somebody pounded on the door.

Harold frowned. Hadn't he told the boyfriend to leave him alone?

"Yeah?" he grunted.

"It's Caroline," came the faint reply.

Caroline? Harold sprang to his feet, baffled. What was she doing *here?*

"Can I come in?" she asked. She sounded nervous.

"Yeah, yeah," Harold mumbled. He dashed forward—nearly stepping on the sick girl's face—and tossed open the flimsy trailer door. It smacked against the outer wall. Harold winced at the sound. He was suddenly very edgy. Something must have gone wrong. . . .

Caroline brushed past him. She was soaked. But she was certainly *dressed* for her part of the plan—wearing only a skimpy miniskirt, a tank top . . . and of all things, high heels. Where had she gotten *those?* But he could worry about that later.

"What's up?" he asked anxiously. "What's going on?"

She didn't reply. Instead she sniffed. Her face shriveled. "What's that *smell?*"

Harold thrust a finger at the girl on the floor. "Look for yourself," he stated flatly. "Now why are you here?"

For a moment Caroline stared down at the dying girl with a look of disgusted fascination. Then she pinched her nostrils and glanced up at Harold. "Duane wasn't around," she said in a nasal voice. "He must have taken off 'cause there's, like, six inches of water in his trailer. I looked all over the place, and I couldn't find him. So I figured I'd look for you instead."

Uh-oh. That wasn't good. Caroline was supposed to be distracting Duane. That was why she was dressed so . . . *suggestively.* And at the same time Larissa was supposed to be going through the rest of the trailer homes and RVs, scouring them for guns,

91

knives, chain saws, whatever. *That* was the plan. Harold was going to stockpile his own little secret cache of weapons before they hit the road tomorrow—so he'd be prepared in case Duane or anyone else tried anything. But now it looked as if the whole operation was turning into a big fiasco.

"What about Larissa?" Harold asked. "Have you seen her?"

Caroline nodded. Her fingers remained over her nose. "Yeah. That's another thing. I bumped into her by the Fig Newtons truck, and she said that she hadn't been able to find any guns at all. She was gonna look for another few minutes, then give up."

Give up? That was ridiculous. Harold opened his mouth to say something—then closed it. He chewed a fingernail. No guns. Yeah, sure. No guns in a trailer park in the middle of the South. For God's sake, he'd seen NRA bumper stickers on at least six RVs. There were guns here, all right. But somebody must have gotten to them first.

"What's wrong?" Caroline asked. "Why don't you—"

She never got to finish the question.

A loud *pop* cut her off. It sounded like a firecracker. Caroline jerked backward and collapsed on top of the dying girl.

Jesus!

Harold instinctively backed away from her—even before he saw the perfectly round black hole above her left eyebrow. His heart plummeted. *She's dead!* He knew to duck down, but he was frozen stiff. He couldn't stop staring at Caroline's beautiful brown eyes, now fixed on the ceiling, glazed and unseeing.

"Dr. Harold Wurf!" a vaguely familiar voice called. "We got you surrounded!"

His eyes widened. The situation suddenly became very clear. Not only had somebody gotten to the guns, somebody was *using* them. But why? He'd fulfilled all his promises. . . .

"Git out here, Doc! With your hands up!"

Duane. Harold dropped to his hands and knees, more angry than scared. He should have known. He just hadn't expected Duane to act up *now,* so soon—

Another shot rang out. A window near the back of the trailer shattered and fell to the linoleum. Rain dripped on the shards of glass.

"You're only making this harder on yourself!" Duane shouted. "We ain't gonna hurt ya!"

Then why are you shooting at me, idiot? Harold fell to his stomach and began slithering toward the back of the trailer, right past the messy heap of bodies. There was no way he was going to let that obese moron kill *him,* too. No way. He had to get to the light switch right by the little bathroom door. If he could turn off the light, then they wouldn't be able to see him.

"We just want to talk," Duane yelled. "We want to know why you're poisoning us. The food here is making everyone sick. People are *dying,* Doc. Was that in your vision, too?"

Harold sneered. So *that* was it. Duane blamed *him* for the epidemic of food poisoning. It figured. Of course, it would never occur to Duane that people could *avoid* getting sick. No. That would be too easy.

Harold crept up under the light switch and rolled over on his back. The little plastic black lever was right above him. All he had to do was jump up and nudge it.

"We know about your plan, Doc!" Duane shouted. "We know you sent Larissa out to find the guns. We know you sent that other slut out to mess with our heads."

Harold paused, his blood running cold.

Larissa. Only three people knew of the plan—and one of them was dead. Larissa must have betrayed him. But why on earth . . . well, he'd figure that out later. Summoning all his strength, he propelled himself off the floor and jabbed at the switch. The tip of his middle finger caught it—and the trailer went black.

Another shot echoed through the air: *pa-ping!*

Christ. Harold swallowed. He rolled over on his stomach again and glanced out the shattered window. He could see the rain and the trees quite clearly now. Good: That meant it was darker in here than it was outside. He reached over and carefully plucked a pointy shard of glass from the pile on the floor. It wasn't any kind of weapon, but it was the best he could do. Dangling it from his fingers, he crawled back past the girls toward the open door.

"Game's over, Doc," Duane barked. "Quit messin' around and git out here."

Harold stole a quick peek outside. Duane was standing in the rain, heatedly whispering to another guy—some tall kid whom Harold barely recognized. So . . . on the plus side, there were only two of them.

But both were armed. Duane had a rifle; the tall kid had a pistol. Harold withdrew his head. Somehow he had to get one of those guns.

". . . if you want," one of them was muttering. "I'm tired of being wet. I'm goin' in."

Going in? There was no time to think. Harold dropped the shard of glass and peeled off his T-shirt, then wrapped the shirt around his hand and used it to grab the glass tightly—creating a makeshift knife.

Footsteps approached. He barely heard them over his own flailing heart. After a silent prayer he pushed himself to his feet and hid next to the door.

The tall boy stepped inside, pistol drawn. He looked first to the left, then to the right.

Harold bit his tongue. The boy wasn't more than a foot away. Harold watched as the guy's eyes fell on Caroline and the other dead girl.

Now!

With his free hand Harold grabbed the boy around the head and clamped his fingers over his mouth, then plunged the pointy edge of the glass into the fleshy area below the boy's sternum. It made a slurping sound. Harold was surprised how easily it went in: like a carving knife through a Thanksgiving turkey. The boy sagged instantly and silently in his arms.

Adrenaline burst through Harold's body. *Ha!* He let go of the shirt and snatched the boy's pistol, allowing him to fall to the linoleum with a clumsy thud.

Whoops. He held his breath. That was loud.

"Freddy?" Duane called. "You all right?"

Once again Harold ducked down and peeked around the side of the door frame. Duane was barely ten feet away, squinting through the rain, his rifle at the ready.

Time to make the final move.

Grasping the pistol with both hands, Harold drew in his breath—then spun through the door, aimed, and fired: *boom!*

There was an explosion, a blinding flash. The gun jerked in Harold's hand. He blinked several times and peered fearfully into the dripping darkness. *Oh, no.* Duane wasn't there. . . .

Then Harold saw him.

Bingo! Duane *was* there—only he wasn't standing. He was writhing in the mud. The rifle lay at his side. Even in the downpour Harold could see black liquid flowing from a hole in Duane's filthy, shredded jeans. It mixed with the rain and mud, spreading in all directions.

So that was that. Two for two. Not bad for a first-time killer. Not bad at all. It was funny: Harold had devoted his life to *prolonging* lives—but in the end terminating them wasn't so bad, either. Of course, Duane wasn't *quite* dead yet. . . .

He chuckled softly and hopped out the door, trotting over to the spot where Duane lay squirming like a fish. For once the cold rain felt quite refreshing on his bare torso. Purifying, in fact. He was going to savor this moment. Yes, yes. This was going to be very sweet. He kicked Duane's rifle aside. But as he stood over the bloated body—with his gun cocked and Duane's quivering jowls in his sights—he just couldn't bring himself to pull the trigger. Not right away, at least. It seemed so anticlimactic. He needed to make this *fun*.

"Get it over with!" Duane barked, cringing.

Oh, please. With a sigh Harold uncocked the pistol and let his arm fall. It wasn't very enjoyable if Duane *wanted* to die.

"Duane, do you know what the Hippocratic oath is?" he asked. The boy simply stared back at him—bewildered and terrified, as if Harold had just threatened him in a foreign language. The puddle of blood under his rump was growing.

"I didn't think so," Harold said. "So let me explain it to you. The Hippocratic oath is a solemn promise made by all doctors when they get their licenses—swearing, in effect, that they will do anything they possibly can to save a human life. I was in the midst of trying to save a human life when you so rudely interrupted me."

Duane swallowed. Doglike pants wheezed from his rubbery lips, but he said nothing.

Harold wrinkled his nose in distaste. "Anyway," he continued, "what I'm trying to *tell* you is that doctors are duty bound to save any life they can. *Any* life. No matter how worthless or fit for the garbage dump it may be. For example . . . if a doctor stumbles upon an injured criminal—say, a criminal who has been shot in the leg—then that doctor has a moral, ethical, and *legal* obligation to help him. Regardless of the crime. Do you understand now?"

A glimmer of hope flashed in Duane's eyes. He

mustered a shaky smile. "So you gonna save me?" he croaked. "That what you sayin'?"

Harold laughed. "Oh, no. Of course not." He cocked the handle of the gun and pointed the barrel at Duane's forehead. "I'm not a doctor, remember? I never received my license."

The smile vanished. "Bu-but . . . I thought—"

"You shouldn't think, Duane," Harold whispered. "It's not your strong suit."

He squeezed the trigger.

**Egyptian Desert,
near El Daheir
Afternoon of March 20**

Sarah had been twisting and turning under the covers for so long that the silk sheets were starting to chafe her skin. Ugly red splotches had appeared on her calves and forearms. But she didn't mind the discomfort. In fact, she was *thankful* for it. The rashes were perfect for enhancing the illusion of illness.

"I think I hear the muezzin," she groaned, even though she didn't. "Shouldn't we go outside to pray now?"

"The muezzin?" Ibrahim mumbled. He'd been sitting at the edge of her mattress for over half an hour, eyeing her worriedly. "No, it must be the rain."

She rubbed her eyes. "The rain?"

"Sarah, are you *certain* you want to join us for prayers?" Ibrahim asked. "The sick are not obligated to pray in the traditional fashion. Allah understands."

"No," she croaked. She pretended to struggle to sit up straight. "I can make it. . . ."

Ibrahim shook his head, gently laying a hand over her legs. "Really, Sarah, it's not important. I admire your spirit, but I think it would be best if you stayed put this afternoon."

"What about praying?" she gasped. "Maybe if I pray, I'll feel better."

"You can pray from bed," Ibrahim stated. He stood up straight, his face creased with concern. "Allah will still hear your prayers. Just try to remain comfortable. I'll be back in no more than five minutes."

"Okay," she muttered, feigning reluctance. She closed her eyes and sank back into the pillows. "But come right back."

"I will."

He hesitated for another moment—then hurried from the room. Sarah held her breath. She strained her ears, listening carefully. Under normal circumstances the guards outside her door would accompany her to the courtyard for prayers.

Did Ibrahim trust her enough to take the guards with him?

There were some mutterings in Arabic. Then a jumble of footsteps clattered away from the door. *Yes!* All three of them were leaving. A smile broke on her face. Ibrahim *did* trust her.

The corridor was clear.

Sarah bolted upright and hopped out from under the covers. Every second counted. For the next five minutes the entire household would be outside praying. She tugged her grubby knapsack out from under the bed and unzipped it with a savage yank. Inside were a pair of jeans, a T-shirt, and sneakers: the outfit she'd worn when Ibrahim had captured her. After hastily dressing she threw the knapsack over her shoulder and tiptoed out into the hall.

As swiftly and quietly as she could she stole through several corridors, down a narrow staircase, and into a long passage that led to the main foyer. It felt so *good* to be wearing her old clothes. They made her feel like *herself* again, like Sarah Levy—not some actress playing a role she didn't even understand.

"*Allah . . . u . . . akhbar . . .*"

The chant of the muezzin echoed across the stone walls. That meant the clock was ticking. She hurtled up the spiral staircase three steps at a time—then tore down the hall and burst into Ibrahim's bedroom. It took her less than five seconds to yank the scroll from under the ebony desk and stuff it into her knapsack.

All she had to do now was get to the stables. She dashed back down the stairs.

Her plan was straightforward: She was going to steal a horse. The only problem was that she wasn't the most skilled rider in the world. She hadn't ridden since she was thirteen, at Camp Seagull. But riding a horse was like riding a bike, wasn't it?

"*Allah . . . u . . . akhbar . . .*" The voices drifted through the rain.

The foul stench of horse manure greeted her nostrils as she skidded around a corner—but at that moment it was the sweetest smell in the world. It was the smell of escape. She plowed right through the open door and into the straw-covered stable.

Then she stopped.

A very angry-looking boy dressed in a stained caftan stood among the horses, glowering at her.

Sarah shook her head, aghast. What was he *doing* here? Didn't Ibrahim say the stable boy vaporized? The horses were supposed to be unattended during prayer—

"Rooch Minhon!" the boy barked. *"Rooch Minhon!"*

She had no idea what that meant—not that it mattered. She took three quick steps across the floor and lunged onto the first horse she saw: a stumpy little brown creature who was bridled but unsaddled.

Ow! She cringed in pain. The pegs of the scroll dug into the small of her back as she fought to straddle the horse. But she *had* to get out of here. Now that she'd been spotted, the clock had reached zero. . . .

"La!" the boy cried.

The horse wheezed and bounced up on its hind legs. Sarah furiously tugged at the rawhide reins. Finally, after several panicked moments, the horse seemed to relax. Sarah kicked its midsection with her heels, steering it toward the stable door.

"Good boy," she murmured. "Good boy."

All at once the animal jumped forward. *Whoa!* The unexpected jolt nearly catapulted her to the ground—but she snatched the reins and somehow managed to stay precariously mounted. An instant later she was flying past the boy and into the rain. The tip of her spine bounced painfully against the horse's body with every stride; the rain and wind whipped at her face. *God!* She'd had no idea horses could move so fast. . . .

And then the horse slowed. Very abruptly.

Sarah swallowed. A twinge of fear flashed through her. What was going on? She shot a quick glance at the horse's legs. *Dammit.* The rain had turned the desert into muck. With every step the horse's hooves sank deep into what looked like

102

quicksand. Sarah dug her heels into his sides, but the horse didn't speed up. It was like trudging through cement.

Raindrops pummeled Sarah's bare arms, chilling her. In desperation she slapped the horse's head. But the blow didn't do a bit of good—

Wait.

Did she hear voices?

A faint cry floated through the pouring rain: *"Yemine, yemine!"*

In horror she glanced over her shoulder. Three horsemen had burst from the stables and were approaching on her right, moving as quickly as possible through the muck. The closest one was probably no more than fifteen yards away. He glared at her—his shiny black eyes clearly visible under a flowing turban.

How did they catch up to me so fast?

She whirled to face front again, but the sudden movement made her head spin.

One of the reins slithered from her grasp.

She teetered off balance. She couldn't sit up straight anymore. An unseen force seemed to be pulling at her, tugging her. . . .

"No!" she screamed. She was falling to the right. She squeezed her eyes shut. "No—"

Something wrenched at her armpit, instantly lifting her off the horse. It hurled her off balance and flipped her through the rain. . . . *Ugh.* Nausea gripped her stomach. She thought she would keep tumbling— but her bottom plopped suddenly and painfully on a hard, wet surface.

Her eyes opened.

She found that she was staring at the back of a turbaned head. The rider had scooped her up onto his horse. She couldn't believe it. But there she was, bouncing on the horse's rear end, her legs dangling off the right side.

"*Dooree!*" the horseman shouted. He wheeled the horse around in the opposite direction, back toward the palace. "*Dooree!*"

Sarah didn't understand him, but she understood one thing: Either she held on for now or she would be trampled in that mush. She grabbed the guy's shoulders and flipped her left leg over the other side of the horse, then leaned forward and hugged his waist as tightly as she could.

"*Hai!*" he cried.

Sarah's head snapped back. She clutched desperately at the horseman's loose robes as the horse charged back toward the palace, its broad back heaving as it lunged through the wet sand. The stable doors grew larger by the second—until they filled her entire field of vision. She couldn't catch her breath. Her mouth was so dry. She was going to pass out. . . .

And there was Ibrahim.

God help me.

He and the two bedroom guards stood in the rain, apart from the rest of the mob that was forming under the stable roof.

He stared at her.

His face was totally impassive, his black eyes dull. The horseman jerked the reins and quickly slowed to a stop in front of him.

"Dismount," Ibrahim commanded.

But Sarah could only lean forward and rest her cheek against the folds of the horseman's white robe. Her eyelids closed. It had all happened so fast. Numb fear filled every crevice of her body. She was simply too exhausted and terrified to move.

"Min fadlach," Ibrahim mumbled.

The next thing she knew, a pair of powerful hands seized her, lifted her from the horse, and dumped her into the mud. Her knees buckled. But she didn't open her eyes. She couldn't; she didn't want to face him. She almost fell flat.

A hand steadied her. Then another hand wrenched the knapsack from her back, taking a shred of her T-shirt with it.

"You lied to me," Ibrahim stated in a toneless voice. "You lied."

Sarah hung her head, defeated. Every last ounce of hope drained away. She'd failed. Nobody would ever learn of the Prophecies; no one would ever be able to crack the code. She would be dead in a matter of seconds. She was certain of it. She had betrayed him.

If she had only believed Elijah in the first place, none of this would have happened. She would have helped Josh decipher the code. Together they could have done it quickly. They could have discovered the truth before those black-robed girls came after them. If she had only had faith in her granduncle . . . maybe the people left on the planet would have a chance. But now it was too late.

"Look at me," Ibrahim breathed.

She couldn't bring herself to do it.

"Look at me."

Summoning what little was left of her will and dignity, she opened her eyes. At the very least she couldn't let herself die like a coward.

"Do you love me?" he asked.

She swallowed. What did he expect her to say?

"This is *my* fault," he whispered. "I was foolish to think you'd converted so fast. But I wanted so desperately to believe you. I'm sorry, Sarah. This has been *my* failure."

She blinked, completely caught off guard. She'd expected an angry tirade, swift and immediate retribution—but an *apology?*

"What are you saying?" she croaked.

"I'm saying that I have to give it more time," he replied. "You need to work at this. Finding your faith won't happen overnight. But someday soon you'll see the truth."

"So . . . so you're not going to punish me?" she stammered.

He sighed deeply. "Of *course* not."

"Then let me go," she cried instinctively. "I'm begging you."

He shook his head. "That I cannot do. I must bring you to Mecca so—"

"No!" she interrupted. "Don't you get it? I'm *not* going with you. I'm never going to convert no matter *what* you say or do. That's why I keep running away—you have no right to keep me here. It's the truth, Ibrahim. Kill me if you have to, but that's how I stand."

Ibrahim's lips trembled. He gazed at her, wearing the exact same expression of bewilderment and hurt as when Sarah had accused him of being with the black-robed girls. Then he nodded to the servant. Before Sarah could react, the servant darted forward and pulled her arms behind her back.

"Hey!" she gasped. She hadn't expected he would really *kill* her. "Stop it!"

But Ibrahim just smiled sadly. She squirmed and kicked. Some kind of smooth rope was being deftly tied around her wrists, binding them together in a firm knot. She tried to jerk free. It was useless.

"I *know* how you stand, Sarah," Ibrahim stated. "And it breaks my heart. But I can't disobey Allah's will. We leave for the Red Sea in the morning. Believe me—as soon as you see the Imam Mahdi, you *will* see the truth. You'll thank me. I know you will. Your body will be purged of all the lies and deceit. Then you and I will be together in paradise."

PART III:

March 21-31

CHAPTER TWELVE

Bethany,
Illinois
Early morning of March 21

I'm standing on a tall cliff, overlooking a vast, gray ocean. The sun is setting on the horizon. My baby is with me. My beautiful baby girl . . .

And Julia is with me, too. Julia, my love.

When I look into my baby's eyes, it's almost like looking into a mirror—a mirror that reflects both Julia and me. The baby has one green eye and one brown. An eye for each of us. The baby has brought us together and made us one.

But Julia seems sad for some reason.

"What's wrong?" I ask.

She shakes her head. Her long dark curls are dazzling in the fading sunlight.

"The Demon," she whispers. "The Demon is coming."

I reach for her, holding her close to me. "No, no," I soothe. "The Demon is gone, remember? We don't have the visions anymore."

A lone tear falls from her eye. "It doesn't matter."

All of a sudden it's night. Very dark. Much too dark. I squeeze Julia tightly to comfort her . . . but she doesn't squeeze back.

And at that moment I hear the footsteps. Yes.

Growing louder. Those unmistakable footsteps. I turn.
  The Demon stands before me.

George jerked upright with a start. He was drenched in sweat. It took him a few moments to realize that he was in bed, in the cabin, that it must be the middle of the night. The rain falling on the roof and windows filled the room with a dull roaring sound. A few embers still glowed in the stone fireplace, bathing the bed in a soft red light.

It was a nightmare. That's all. Just chill.

George flopped back in bed. Damn. He sighed and ran a hand over his moist forehead, brushing the hair out of his eyes. Man, could he go for a smoke right now. Or a beer. Anything to calm his nerves. What a freak-out. He hadn't had a nightmare like that in a long, long time. He hadn't seen that baby or the Demon in weeks, not since his last vision. He'd almost forgotten about all that. . . .

But not quite.

No. He rolled over on his side. Julia lay beside him under the quilt, her chest rising slowly and evenly in the steady rhythm of deep sleep.

God, she was beautiful.

He reached out and ran a hand through her curls. No, he hadn't forgotten about the baby. *That* vision seemed to take on new meaning ever since that night a week ago . . . ever since he had suddenly found himself kissing Julia—first softly, then with greater fervor and desire . . . until they'd made love in a frenzy of passion that he could never have dreamed or imagined possible.

Nothing so perfect can be real.

"George?" Julia murmured. She squirmed a little, but her eyes remained closed. "Are you okay?"

He smiled. "Yeah," he whispered. "I just had a nightmare. Go back to sleep."

She nodded. Within seconds she was dozing again.

George lay perfectly still for a moment, staring at her. He could lie like this until he died. Seriously. If he melted into one of those puddles of black goo right now, he would still feel as if his life was worth something. All the crap he'd put up with for the past sixteen years—the shuffling around to different foster homes, his stupid friends, the crime, the arrests—none of it meant a damn thing in the face of what he shared with Julia.

Now I finally understand why people write those lame love songs, he thought with a grin.

Yup. Being in love was pretty sweet. So was *making* love. Pretty sweet indeed. It was kind of funny: He'd never thought about having sex in terms of "making love." It was always "doing the nasty," or "gettin' some," or . . . well, worse. But with Julia—

A jagged bolt of lightning flashed outside the window.

For an instant it illuminated the cabin and the lake in a harsh blue-white glow.

George's brow furrowed. *Hmmm.* His eyes must have been playing tricks on him. He didn't see any trees out there. All he saw was water. The lake wasn't *that* close. . . .

There was a deafening crack of thunder.

Frowning, he hopped out of bed and tiptoed over to the window.

"George?" Julia moaned. "What's—"

"Jesus!" he cried.

Horror gripped him.

The lake *was* that close. It was halfway up the freaking side of the cabin. When the hell had *that* happened?

"George?" Julia asked again, suddenly sounding very alert.

"We gotta get out of here," George gasped.

For a second he couldn't move. He whirled around—dashing first for his jeans on the floor, then for the keys to the pickup truck all at once. He nearly fell flat on his face. He couldn't think straight. Was this another nightmare? It had to be. He was too damn scared.

"Come on!" he shouted. "Get up!"

Julia sat upright in bed, rubbing her puffy eyes. "What's going on?"

"I—I don't know," he stammered, struggling to zip up his pants. His hands were shaking. "The lake musta flooded overnight. We gotta split. *Now!*"

"Now?" Julia shook her head, a look of utter confusion on her face. "But . . ."

George took a step into the kitchen and found himself splashing into a puddle. His feet were suddenly freezing. He looked down. *Crap!* He stood ankle deep in black water—water that covered half the floor and was probably rising fast.

"Come on, Julia!" he yelled. He sloshed over to the keys and snatched them off the top of the little refrigerator, then jumped back into the main room. "Get out of bed."

But Julia was already stumbling around the cabin, desperately trying to put on her clothes. George shook his head. They couldn't waste any time. He grabbed her arm and rushed her toward the door. They'd be able to dress later.

"Hopefully the truck will start," George whispered shakily, trying to tug her along. "It's got pretty good traction in the mud. . . ."

They burst out into the rain—and stopped.

They couldn't go any farther.

The lake had not only flooded, it had blocked the cabin from the main road. A raging river littered with twigs and branches stood between them and any hope of escape. And as far as the truck was concerned, only the back end of the flatbed was visible—jutting out of the frothy water at a forty-five-degree angle. The front end was completely submerged.

It was gone. For good.

They were trapped.

"Oh, my God," Julia whispered. She turned to George, her dark eyes brimming with tears. "We're gonna die."

CHAPTER
THIRTEEN

It took Harold three days to find Larissa. When he did, she was cowering in the back of the destroyed ambulance in a puddle of murky brown water, half starved and out of her mind. Her clothes were green from mildew. She must have been cooped up in there since Friday—the day Harold nailed the bodies of Duane and Freddy to the back of the Fig Newtons truck. It was just a pleasant reminder of what would happen to those who refused to believe in him.

Of course, hardly anyone refused to believe in him now.

Harold stood beside Larissa and calmly chewed one of the Fig Newtons. He wanted to put her at ease. The pistol tucked into his belt was probably making her nervous. She was shivering. Her eyes were wide. Rain clattered on the roof.

"You're going to kill me, aren't you?" she breathed.

He shook his head. "No, Larissa," he said. His mouth was full. He forced the rest of the cookie down his throat in one gulp. "I'm not going to kill you. The Healer doesn't kill, remember? The Healer protects his flock."

114

Her eyes widened. "B-but aren't you mad? I mean—"

"I just want to know *why*, Larissa," he interrupted gently. "Every savior has his Judas. I just never expected it would be *you*. You were the very first one I saved. Haven't I fulfilled all my promises, all my visions?"

She nodded feverishly. Her head bobbed up and down like a yo-yo.

"When you came to me, didn't I heal you?"

"Yes," she breathed.

"When the flock went hungry, didn't I lead them to pasture?"

Her eyes moistened. "Yes."

"I promised food and shelter, and I delivered them."

"I know, I know." Tears began to flow down her cheeks.

Like putty in my hands, he thought delightedly. "So why the betrayal?"

"I was jealous, okay?" she shrieked. "*I* was the one who loved you first, remember? I didn't want to hurt you, really. I swear." She sniffed and wiped her eyes. "I only wanted to hurt Caroline. The way she threw herself at you—it made me sick. I wanted to kill her."

Harold frowned. The words shocked him. If Caroline made her angry, why hadn't she *said* anything? He had assumed that she *enjoyed* the kinky little arrangement in the ambulance.

But of course . . . she was too *scared* of him to say anything. She didn't want to displease him, at least not to his face. So she felt compelled to go behind his back.

"Why did you tell Duane what I was planning?" he asked.

115

She shook her head miserably. "I knew he'd never kill you, Harold," she sobbed. "Nothing can kill you. . . ."

He cocked his eyebrow. "Come on, Larissa," he scolded in a playful, singsong voice. "You must have had a reason."

But she was weeping uncontrollably now. "Please, Harold. I'm sorry. I'm so sorry. The rain, all the rain—it's making me nuts. I can't think straight. I love you. I've never loved anyone like you. I'd give my soul to you if I could."

"Okay." He patted her knee, then left. *Whew.* This girl was a prime candidate for institutionalization. But at least he knew that she would never betray him again. She was too terrified.

Someday soon he'd kill her, of course.

For now, however, he was ready to resume the journey north.

One, two, three days.

Forty miles, two vaporizations, nineteen more cases of food poisoning.

In the town of Sweetwater, Harold decided to call a meeting to soothe the troubled flock. They were nearing the promised land, he assured them. He knew the rain was wearing them down. He knew they were hungry and sick; he knew they were frightened of watching their companions melt away into black puddles. *He* was frightened, too. But in the face of fear, they had to remain strong. They had to fight temptation and selfishness. Faith would see them through. Because they were a *family*, the sons and

116

daughters of a proud parent—a parent who would provide salvation so long as they believed in him.

That seemed to shut them up for a while.

Only fifteen more miles to Amarillo! One day's journey!

Harold decided to celebrate by breaking into the Marriot on Interstate 27. His parents had taken him to the restaurant there on his eighth birthday. It hadn't changed a bit in twelve years: polyester carpeting, puke yellow wallpaper, the works. But it was a fine place. There was plenty of nonperishable food still left in the enormous pantry, and the restaurant was well stocked with a wide assortment of liquors. Harold planted himself on a stool at the bar in front of a bottle of eighteen-year-old, single-malt scotch. About twenty kids joined him there for the party. For a while, anyway, the rain outside the windows seemed very far away. . . .

He was just beginning to enjoy himself when a skinny, pockmarked boy slammed a beer glass down in front of him.

"My name's Jake," the boy slurred, breathing stale booze into Harold's face. His damp T-shirt reeked of fungus. "I've wanted to talk to you for a long time."

Wonderful, Harold thought.

"You know why?" Jake smiled crookedly.

Harold rolled his eyes. He wasn't in the mood to play Messiah at the moment. "No. Enlighten me."

"I think you're full of crap. I think you're a fraud."

A few teenagers near them gasped.

But Harold just smiled back. "Why's that?"

"If you got all these powers, why can't you stop the rain?" He slapped his own chest. "My shirt is practically rotting off my body!"

The bar was suddenly very quiet.

"The rain will stop soon enough," Harold stated calmly.

"Oh, yeah?" Jake growled. "You sure about that?"

Harold nodded. He figured the word *soon* was an appropriately ambiguous term. After all, it had been raining for about four straight weeks. How much longer could it last?

Jake kept glaring at him. "And what about the meltin' sickness, huh? If you're some kinda healer, how come you can't heal *that?*"

"Look, Jake, why don't you join me for a drink?" Harold suggested.

"'Cause I gotta take a piss." Jake flashed what was probably supposed to be a menacing grin, then he staggered off through the crowd in search of the bathroom. He left his beer glass on the bar. "Goddamn fraud," he was mumbling. "Goddamn . . ."

The teenagers began to whisper among themselves.

Harold frowned. He couldn't let this disrespect go unpunished; otherwise he would appear weak. So what could he do? He thought for a moment, then remembered the packet of powdered morphine he'd taken from the ambulance. Of course. It was still stuffed into the front pocket of his jeans, if memory served him correctly. His fingers felt for it . . . yes, there it was. It contained enough morphine to kill several elephants.

That would do quite nicely.

118

He quickly withdrew the packet and tore it open, coughing to mask the sound. Then he stood up and stretched, leaning against the bar with his hands behind his back. When nobody was looking, he surreptitiously slipped the powder into Jake's beer. Once it was all gone, Harold crumpled the empty packet and stuffed it back into his pocket.

A minute later Jake returned to the bar.

"You still here?" he barked at Harold. He snatched up his glass and chugged the rest of his beer in one sloppy gulp. Then he belched loudly.

Harold smiled. He took a deep breath. "I'd like to have your attention, please!" he announced to the crowd. "Everybody! Listen up!"

The teenagers fell silent. Jake gaped at him.

"This boy by my side is a nonbeliever. As you know, all nonbelievers die. So this boy will die tonight. Very soon. That is all." He sat back down and picked up his scotch.

Jake clamped a hand down on his shoulder. "What the hell are you talkin' about?"

Harold shrugged.

Ten minutes later Jake collapsed onto the floor. He twitched a few times, then turned blue. Harold took one last swig and invited everyone to gather around Jake's flaccid body.

"I told you he would die, didn't I?" Harold asked, beaming at the stunned faces.

Jake's tongue was sticking out of his mouth. It was purple. His eyes were open. White mucus dribbled from his lips and onto his chin.

"Yes, yes. He's dead, all right. It makes you wonder

why people still question my powers, doesn't it?"

Nobody asked Harold about the rain or the vaporizations after that.

The long journey was finally coming to a close.

Harold rubbed his eyes. Was it true? Could he really see the old red silo jutting over the wheat field, the cozy wood frame house at the end of the muddy road? Even in the drizzle the place looked beautiful. For a moment he thought he might burst into tears.

How long had it been since he'd come home? Not since September, in another era, another lifetime. He sprinted ahead of the flock on the muddy road, kicking up grime under his heels as he ran.

Memories of Ma and Pop came flooding back, unbidden. But they didn't cause him any sadness. No, he'd been happy here. His parents had treated him like the genius he truly was. And so would his flock. The circle was complete.

I made it. All my wishes come true.

They really did, didn't they? More than once in the past few weeks he'd found himself thinking about what Duane said the day he crashed the ambulance: "Nobody's *this* damn lucky."

Duane was absolutely right.

But something deeper than luck was operating here—something mysterious and profound. What else could explain the miraculous string of events? Harold had never been a believer in the divine, but he had little doubt that some sort of blessing was shining down upon him.

He stopped dead in his tracks.

Something really *was* shining down upon him.

He looked up at the sky. *My God!*

The rain was clearing! A few drops still fell to the earth, but he could see patches of blue. And there, high above him . . . sporadically poking through the thinning cloud cover . . . he could almost see it . . .

The sun.

His lips spread in a huge smile. For a moment he just stood in the road, his face tilted skyward, eyes closed, basking in the long-forgotten glow. A heavy, invisible blanket seemed to lift from his body. Never had the sun's rays felt so warm, so comforting. He *knew* the rain had to end! He glanced back at the flock.

But none of them were looking at the sky. They were all looking at *him*.

They thought he was responsible.

Am I?

With the sun blazing down at him and those awestruck faces gazing into his own, Harold realized the truth. All the good luck, the defeat of his enemies, his unending stream of successes: All of it finally made sense. In a vivid flash he saw his life as a climb up a steep wall—a wall that had obscured the truth until this very moment. But he had finally reached the top. He was finally able to glimpse the other side, to glimpse reality.

He *was* responsible.

He'd been greeted with signs and with wonders. The long rain was over. He'd reached the promised land.

He truly *was* the Healer.

"You're a holy man!" a voice cried. "Sent from heaven!"

I am, Harold realized. *I really am.*

The Third Lunar Cycle

"Black moon, Lilith," Naamah chanted under her breath. "Sister darkest . . ."

She stared down at the dam from the hovering helicopter, luxuriating in the sunlight that flowed through the windows. For the first time in more than a month the sun was showing its face. Just as the Prophecies had foretold.

"Black moon, Lilith, Mare of Night . . ."

The month of rain had served the Lilum well. Other plagues would strike the planet in the coming lunar cycles . . . and those, too, would serve Naamah and her sisters. But the rain was particularly sweet. It had blocked the sun's rays, weakening the second sight of the Visionaries. It had caused the oceans to rise.

"Don't you think we should leave?" Captain Hillerman asked anxiously.

Naamah smiled. "Soon," she murmured. She wanted to see her work with her own eyes.

It was the day of the flood. The Prophecies said so.

In a matter of minutes an earthquake under the Red Sea would unleash a flood—at the very moment the dam exploded. Water would sweep across the earth in both directions, creating a catastrophe so devastating that the Suez Canal would be destroyed, that every survivor in the Nile delta would be drowned, and that all access to and from the Sinai Peninsula would be blocked.

That meant anyone trying to get to Africa from Israel would be unable to do so.

As of today Israel would be sealed off on all sides—a 7,992-square-mile prison.

Naamah's smile widened.

When she'd first learned that Elijah Levy's scroll was missing, she'd admittedly been perturbed. But now it didn't matter. Whoever had the scroll would be trapped in Israel. The Mediterranean sealed off the west. The Lilum sealed off the north and east in a human blockade: hunting down soldiers, setting up roadblocks, exterminating every single person who tried to pass. Three of four borders were contained.

And soon, very soon the flood would seal the fourth.

Naamah glanced at the cockpit clock. Almost time! Three . . . two . . . one . . .

Her head jerked up. There it went. . . . The dam was instantly ablaze in a checkerboard pattern of silent white flashes. In seeming slow motion large rectangular chunks of the curved concrete wall began to fall forward, tumbling like a house of cards. They splashed into the Nile amid a cloud of rubble and dust—

A blast wave slammed the helicopter.

Naamah was thrown forward in her seat. The small pod jerked violently. Captain Hillerman fought with the controls. But Naamah was not afraid. Her eyes glazed over with delight as a frothy tidal wave surged forward from Lake Nasser and obliterated the last standing remnants of the dam, blanketing the earth in a newborn sea.

Checkmate.

Whoever had taken that scroll could never conceive of the awesome power of the Lilum.

The Lilum had changed the face of the earth in order to ensure the scroll's destruction.

Naamah laughed. Her work was done here. It was time to cross the ocean. It was time to empower the Healer, the false prophet who would draw the Visionaries into a trap before they could ever set eyes upon the Chosen One. . . .

CHAPTER FOURTEEN

Egyptian Desert,
near Quseir
Morning of March 27

Can't this thing go any faster? Sarah wondered. She didn't think she'd ever felt more sick in her life. *If we don't get there soon, I know I'm gonna vomit. . . .*

It figured that Ibrahim would use a horse and buggy to travel hundreds of miles through a desert that had basically turned to quicksand. It was totally stupid and senseless, like every other decision he made. The carriage kept rocking back and forth on its rickety little wheels—and even when it was completely caught in the sludge, it still shimmied enough to make her nauseous. Plus, as if *that* weren't bad enough, it was so dark in here that she could barely see. No direct light penetrated the thick shroud of tapestries. She could hardly *breathe,* the air was so stale. Why hadn't he put any windows in this goddamn thing?

She shook her head. She knew she shouldn't get agitated. After all, nothing mattered anymore. Nothing. She and everyone else were doomed. But she couldn't help herself. She found she was irate. If the Al-Saif family could afford eight houses and a private yacht, they could afford *one* off-road vehicle. Then she and Ibrahim would have reached the Red Sea in *one* day instead of seven. Then they wouldn't be slogging through this miserable rain—

The carriage suddenly tilted to the right.

"Sarah!" Ibrahim cried. His voice sounded muffled through the cloth walls. "It's a miracle! You must see for yourself!"

For a few seconds the carriage tipped so far that Sarah thought it would fall on its side. She clutched at the padded shackles around her ankles, fighting to keep her balance—but it was nearly impossible. What was Ibrahim *doing?* If he was trying to torture her, he was doing an excellent job. For God's sake, she couldn't hang on. . . .

And then it leveled off and jerked to a stop.

Sarah collapsed back against some pillows. *Finally.* But if they weren't moving, they were probably stuck again.

"Come out here!" Ibrahim was yelling. "Come on!"

You have to let me off my leash first, she thought bitterly.

"Sarah?"

She made a face. Was he suffering from brain damage? If he wanted her to come out, then *he* was going to have to come in here to unlock these shackles. And why was he even *talking* to her? She'd been ignoring him for the entire journey. She hadn't said more than ten words to him since they'd left—not a complete sentence in an entire week. She was pretty proud of herself. But it was a pleasure to keep her mouth shut in his presence. He never listened, anyway. If he insisted on marrying her, he was going to have to marry a mute.

The front curtain flew open. "I'm sorry—"

"Hey!" she interrupted. He was shining a flash-light in her face; there was a blinding white glare. "Stop it! Turn that off!"

Ibrahim laughed. "Turn it off? Sarah, I can't turn it off."

"Why the hell not?" she barked.

"It's not in my control, Sarah," he said. "It's the sun."

The curtain flopped back down. Once again the carriage was dark.

The sun? She blinked a few times, abruptly forgetting her anger. "Are you serious?"

Ibrahim knelt beside her and pulled a key from his robes. "Of course I am. And I'm glad you've decided to talk to me again." He began unlocking the iron clamps around her wrists. "This is a very auspicious moment. I don't think it's an accident that Allah has allowed the sun to shine on the very day we sail for Jiddah."

The very day.

The words triggered a rapid succession of memories—and all at once she gasped.

"Ibrahim, what's the date?" she demanded.

He glanced up at her, puzzled. "The twenty-seventh of March. Why do—"

"That's it!" she cried. "Three, twenty-seven, ninety-nine!"

Ibrahim's eyes narrowed. "Pardon?"

"The date in the scroll!" She shook her head, not knowing whether she felt horrified or ecstatic. "Don't you get it, Ibrahim? You're *right*. It's *not* an accident that the sun is shining. The scroll predicted it! Don't you remember? I showed you the

127

date: three, twenty-seven, ninety-nine. It can't be a coincidence."

"It can't?" Ibrahim snorted, then unlocked the last of her shackles. "Of course it can."

"How can you say that?" she protested. "It *has* to mean something."

He stood, gazing at her blankly. "I don't think so."

"Well, what about the number three?" She jumped up after him. Her legs felt amazingly light now that they were free from the burden of heavy chains. She nearly slammed her head into the ceiling. "Or the number ninety-nine? The scroll mentioned the number ninety-nine! It has to be the month and the year! This is the year ninety-nine!"

Ibrahim pushed through the curtain and out into the blazing sunshine. "Ninety-nine," he mused. "Perhaps it refers to the ninety-nine names of Allah. Have you ever considered *that?*"

"Oh, come *on*," she moaned in frustration. There was simply no talking to a fanatic like Ibrahim; *everything* supported his beliefs. "Just look at—"

"Sarah, enough!" he barked. He spun to face her. "We're going to see the *Imam Mahdi*. I will hear *no* more talk of the scroll. Is that clear?"

She threw her hands in the air. "If you don't want me to talk about the scroll, then why did you take it with us? Huh? I saw you shove it into your bag. Why?"

His face softened. "So that one day you can see its folly," he replied. He sounded as if he were talking to a stupid but much loved child. "Now come."

Folly? She had a sudden urge to punch him. But it

128

wouldn't do a bit of good. Nothing would. Shielding her eyes from the sun, she climbed after him into the hot desert sand and followed him up a steep, rocky incline to the crest of a ridge.

"Where are we going?" she demanded.

"I want you to see the view," he explained, carefully picking his way to the top. "It's spectacular. From up here you can see my parents' yacht at the port of Quseir. You can see far across the Red Sea. And in the other direction you can see the beginnings of the Nile delta."

Sarah nearly screamed. She was on the verge of proving the scroll's authenticity—and he wanted to go sightseeing. "Look, Ibrahim, I think today is important. I think something big is going to happen—"

"*La!*" he suddenly cried. "My boat! It's gone!"

Sarah bit her lip. *Gone?* Now *this* was an interesting development.

"My boat!"

She scurried up beside him. *Wow.* She hadn't realized how high they were. An enormous coastline lay far below them, maybe a mile from the base of the ridge. Blue water stretched to the horizon, meeting the sky in a white haze. The surface was dotted with tiny boats. But there was no big yacht. And off to the left stood the beginnings of a city. It looked strange, though. It seemed to start in the *middle* of the Red Sea. She could clearly see chimneys and towers and roofs poking out from the waves.

"Th-there should be a port," Ibrahim stammered. His dark skin seemed to have turned slightly greenish. "The rain must have flooded it."

Of course it did, Sarah thought, her excitement growing. "Ibrahim, don't you get it?" she cried. "The scroll predicted this! It said that the waters would rise!"

He whirled around. "Why do you insist on—" He broke off in midsentence.

"Why do I insist on *what?*"

Ibrahim just shook his head. Now he wasn't even looking at her. He was squinting at something off in the distance, over her shoulder—in the direction of the desert.

"Aswan," he whispered.

Sarah frowned, then turned to look. Her eyes narrowed. For a moment she thought that the heat waves were playing tricks on her vision. A flat black line had appeared on the horizon, right where the sand began to give way to sporadic bits of greenery. She blinked, expecting the line to disappear. It didn't. It *grew,* covering more and more ground, inching its way toward the base of the ridge.

"What *is* that?" she asked.

He shook his head again. "The—the dam," he stammered.

"The *what?*" she snapped impatiently. As the blackness drew closer she could see that its surface was vaguely uneven. . . .

Sarah sucked in her breath. Water. It was water. The desert was *flooding.* And she noticed something else, too. A lone black cloud sat perched at the spot where the blackness ended and the sky began.

Her impatience melted away.

It wasn't a rain cloud. It was . . .

An explosion?

A deafening peal of thunder shattered her thoughts.

She turned to Ibrahim just long enough to see the panic in his eyes—and the next instant she found herself being hurtled to the ground.

"Ibrahim!" she cried.

Her face scraped against the hot crystals of sand. Some unseen force shook the earth. It took her a moment to realize that the entire *ridge* was moving. Terror washed over her. She clutched at a nearby rock, eyes wide. But the movement was so intense that she couldn't get ahold of anything solid.

"Earthquake!" Ibrahim gasped. "Don't move!"

He was lying right beside her, his hands clamped over his head. Strangely, even in the upheaval, he looked as if he were lying perfectly still. In horror Sarah realized that everything was vibrating at once, so it looked as if nothing were moving at all. She kept her gaze pinned to Ibrahim's black hair. The rumbling thunder grew louder. She could hear the hillside crumbling around them.

Please, God, let me live, she prayed frantically. Never before had she felt so powerless. *Please, God, let me live. I know I've never prayed before; I know I've never believed in you, but I'm going to change. The scroll made me change. . . .*

And then the ground stopped shaking.

Sarah blinked.

She held her breath. The rumble had ceased. The air was still. As suddenly as the earthquake had started, it ended. She couldn't tell how much time had passed—a minute or twenty minutes—but it was over.

A bird chirped overhead.

Ibrahim stood and brushed the dirt and sand off his white robes. "Be careful," he warned in a businesslike manner. "There may be aftershocks."

She nodded, unable to speak.

That's it?

It was incredible. Her prayers had been answered! Slowly, very slowly, she pushed herself up beside him and looked at her surroundings.

No . . .

At first she thought she was having some sort of hysterical reaction to an overload of stress. Something in her brain must have snapped. She was hallucinating. The landscape that greeted her eyes was too alien, too improbable.

The desert was gone.

It had been completely smothered in a filthy brown deluge. There was no trace of any life. On the eastern slope the sea level had risen dramatically. A large part of the coast was missing. A few wrecked boats floundered in the swirling whitecaps, but they were already sinking below the waves.

Sarah peered to her left, then her right. The blue water met the brown on either side of the ridge in a rough smudge of gray.

That meant she wasn't standing on a ridge anymore.

She was standing on an *island*—a rocky desert island in a string of similar islands: tall peaks in a vast and violent body of water that stretched in all directions as far as she could see.

Ibrahim sank to his knees. "Why?" he cried, shaking his fists at the sky. "What have I done, Lord? What have I *done?*"

Sarah couldn't respond to that. But a thought occurred to her. Her prayers really *had* been answered. She'd been allowed to live.

And it looked as though she was going to live out the rest of her very short life stranded here with Ibrahim, the scroll, and the collapsed ruins of an extremely expensive carriage.

Sana couldn't respond to that, but she thought so—
because, to her. Her prayers really had been answered.
She'd been allowed to live.

And... *rather*, though she was afraid to live
out the rest of her very short life trapped bare with
Ibrahim, the scroll... and she collapsed ruins of an
extremely expensive carriage.